CAT DANCER

ALSO BY SHAW COLLINS

CASSIA LEMON MYSTERIES

———

www.ShawCollins.com

SHAW COLLINS

CAT DANCER

A Cassia Lemon Mystery

GREENLEES
PUBLISHING

Published by Greenlees Publishing, contact@greenleespublishing.com

eBook ISBN-13: 978-1-951098-18-6

Paperback ISBN-13: 978-1-951098-23-0

Large Print Paperback ISBN-13: 978-1-951098-24-7

Artwork by Kudryashka, Deposit Photos

To Pumpkin,
as loud as you can be sometimes...

CHAPTER 1

Cassia Lemon, known as Cat to her friends, sat at one of the window booths of Smith's Deli and Diner and sipped her coffee. The late afternoon sun angled down and bathed the whole diner in a golden light, fitting for the beautiful dog-days-of-summer weather waiting outside. Brown leaves blew down the street, but today it was warm enough to wear shorts.

Really tight cop shorts to be exact.

Cassia angled her body to see out the window so it wouldn't look obvious she was staring, but it gave her an uncomfortable crick in her neck. The vinyl seat complained with a squeak as she shifted to find a better position. The squeak echoed in the emptiness of the diner behind her, but she glanced back anyhow to make sure no one had come in from the kitchen where the rest of the crew were still banging around and cleaning for the night.

The diner's seating area stood empty. The chairs were flipped on top of their tables, and the floor shone where it was not yet dry from Cassia's mopping.

Cassia turned back to the window.

Outside, Sheriff Andrews walked along the line of parked

1

cars on Main Street, Forgotten Valley, Minnesota. It was a Saturday, at 4:45 pm. The meters had to be on for fifteen more minutes. The city council had just passed Saturday enforcement, and Sheriff Andrews was a stickler for the rules.

He wore the summer uniform of the sheriff's department, which in his case was blue shorts with a tuxedo stripe up the side, the taut fabric straining on his muscular thighs, and a tight shirt so closely fitting to his massive pecs that the sheriff's badge stuck out like an errant button.

The only thing he had on that was not two sizes too small was his holster. He could have been on stage at a Mr. Universe competition.

Or a lady's club.

He stood on the sidewalk on the far side of the street and eyed the cars and their meters, just waiting for one wrong move.

Or one expired meter.

Cassia giggled. He looked like a boot camp sergeant in one of the war movies, primed to yell at the first plebe who stepped out of line.

She pulled out her phone and placed it on the table. It read 4:46 pm. Fourteen more minutes of the Sheriff Andrews show.

Cassia tipped her cup, draining the last of her coffee. There was more in the pot behind her, but she was loath to leave her seat.

She glanced back out the window. Sheriff Andrews had left the far side of the street and now stood right in front of the diner window. Did he not see her sitting right there?

"I like it best when he bends down to chalk the tires," Genevieve said in Cassia's ear as she also stared at Sheriff Andrews. Cassia jumped and her coffee cup clattered out of her hand. Genevieve reached over and grabbed it before it could hit the floor, then pushed Cassia further into the booth so she could sit next to her.

2

"Jeez, don't scare me like that," Cassia said.

"Shush, he'll hear us," Genevieve said.

"Through the glass? Can't he just see us anyhow?" Cassia said, but she lowered her voice anyhow. The two of them stared at the sheriff doing his duty.

"I don't think he sees anything but meters right now, and for the next," Genevieve looked at Cassia's phone, "ten minutes." Even in her baby blue waitress uniform, Genevieve exuded coolness. Her manga styled, asymmetrical spiked blue hair and trendy boots lined with thick silver buckles somehow made it all work. It made Cassia self-conscious of her own simple brown hair and fashion sense that was mostly old T-shirts and thrift shop specials. She was going to change that one of these days.

"Hunting wabbits out there?" Trent asked as he slid into the seat across from them. His dark curls were damp with sweat, but he looked happy and satisfied, as he should. He owned the place, and it had been packed today.

"The wascalliest of wabbits," Genevieve said, doing an amazingly good impression of the cartoon hunter.

The three of them stared out the window and watched Sheriff Andrews, the voice of law and order in Forgotten Valley, make sure everything was as it should be. Cassia's cell phone lit up with an alarm at 5 pm sharp, just as Sheriff Andrews took one last look down the street and walked off to his station one street over.

They sighed in unison.

"Well, that was fun," Trent said as he rose from the booth. "I'm off to run errands."

"A date?" Genevieve asked. She smirked at him.

"That's none of your business, and no," Trent said as he cocked a finger gun at Genevieve and backed up. "Lock up?"

"Sure," Genevieve said. She waited until he'd walked out

the front door and then turned to Cassia. "It's definitely a date."

"How do you know?" Cassia asked as she stared at her empty coffee cup.

"Because it's the only reason he wouldn't hang out for another hour." Genevieve followed Cassia's eyes. "No more coffee here. Let's go do something fun," she said as she grabbed Cassia's cup from the table as she stood.

Only hesitating for a moment, Cassia followed.

———

Genevieve stood with her hands on her hips, surveying the mess that was Cassia's bedroom, or rather the clothes that lay on every surface of the hotel-room-like furnishings of the luxuriously appointed room. The large four-poster walnut bed, with two matching end tables and lamps, sat in a sea of boxes Cassia had not unpacked yet. She'd been waiting to decide if she was going to move bedrooms or not.

Now, old shirts, with only a single hole or two, decorated the boxes, along with faded jeans, one nice pair of new jeans but so big that they required the use of Cassia's only and rather ugly brown leather belt, lots of shorts, a few oddball hats and an impressive collection of sandals, only slightly used.

The nicest shirt in the collection, a red silky piece Cassia thought sophisticated, now draped over a lampshade, giving the room an atmospheric red glow. Genevieve had rejected it immediately.

The only place untouched was Miss Mansfield's perch on the highest stack of boxes. The sleek black cat watched the proceedings below her, her golden eyes taking it all in.

Cassia sat on the bed, half hidden under clothes. She considered slipping under the pile completely and seeing if

Genevieve would give up and leave. The determination burning in Genevieve's eyes was fearsome indeed.

"Cat, only you would have this many clothes and actually have nothing to wear," Genevieve said. Her mouth turned down in disapproval.

"I can *wear* all of them," Cassia said. Was that a whine in her voice? It was most definitely a whine. Cassia flopped over on the bed, jostling the clothes. "They worked perfectly fine at school."

"What? While you were buried in the library or some remote mountaintop astronomy observatory? This is real life," Genevieve said distractedly as she dug through a moving box one more time in the hopes something decent would magically appear, even though she had just checked it five minutes ago.

"That was real life," Cassia muttered. She didn't bother getting up to help. Genevieve had rejected every one of her suggestions. She'd brought this turn of events on herself, Cassia knew. She'd had the bright idea to ask Genevieve to help her with her fashion sense and the girl had lit up like a Christmas tree and made a beeline for Cassia's clothes once they got back to the Mandress mansion.

"This can't be that fancy a place. It's just a dance studio, right?" Cassia asked while she stared at the ceiling.

"It could be," Genevieve answered, her voice muffled as she dug deep in the tall box. "New businesses are rare around here, and they said they're going to have balls and parties on the weekends, too. Perfect timing for those of us dying for something fun to do in the winter."

"Don't say that word," Cassia said with a groan.

"What? Parties?" Genevieve popped up, a ratty hand-knit hat somehow stuck on her head from digging in the clothes.

"No, the other word."

"Winter?"

"Ugh! I said, don't say that word," Cassia said. She rolled over on the bed and put her hands over her head.

Winter really was not her thing. Cassia missed California more than she thought possible. She'd only been in Forgotten Valley, Minnesota, for a month but a few of those weeks had been colder than she could ever remember, and there were apparently four or five more months of it coming. This was going to be the longest year of her young life.

They'd had a reprieve these last few days with the warmer weather, but Cassia knew that was not going to last. She groaned.

"Think of it as an opportunity to buy some new clothes. Warmer ones," Genevieve said. "Prettier ones too." Genevieve gingerly held up an old T-shirt with a brewery logo on it by her fingertips. "What is this?"

Cassia rolled over to look at the shirt. "Hey, that's a famous place," Cassia said.

"Ever been there?" Genevieve asked.

"No. What's that got to do with it?"

Genevieve didn't bother to answer as she threw the shirt back in the box. She sat down on the bed next to Cassia.

Cassia sat up. "You know, shopping would be a lot easier if we would ever get that reward money."

"Agreed. It's been weeks already."

Cassia and Genevieve had been promised reward money for helping catch a famous art thief, or more honestly, just avoiding being killed by her crazy minion, but like all things regarding government, it was taking forever. The same was true for getting some funds from Aunt Mildred's estate. The art thief had been posing as Aunt Mildred's housekeeper and had really managed to put a wrench in everything, and now Cassia had to clean up the mess.

"Any word on when you're going to get the stuff from the

warehouse back?" Genevieve asked, referring to the stolen house items the investigators had found.

"I guess I can get them any time, but I can't afford a truck right now. It sounds like a lot of stuff."

"Yeah, this is a mansion after all," Genevieve said, giving Cassia a slow-motion punch to the upper arm. "Poor little rich girl."

"Hey, stop it." Cassia said, protesting.

"Okay, okay. But we are going to have to do something about tonight. You never get a second chance at a first impression, and I've been looking forward to going to this opening for weeks." She gave Cassia a devious smile.

———

Genevieve's 1986 midnight blue Honda Accord zipped down the narrow two-lane road, going faster than Cassia thought safe. The sun had long ago set and only the car's old and dim headlights provided light on the narrow road. The beams bounced off the thick pine trees that crowded the northern Minnesota road. At least no deer had appeared... yet. Cassia doubted the car or the deer would survive a collision at the speed they were going.

Grasping the handle above the window, Cassia stared at Genevieve driving.

"Don't even say it," Genevieve said, not bothering to look back.

"Say what?" Cassia said, feigning ignorance. She'd been weighing whether asking Genevieve to slow down would make it worse and goad Genevieve into driving even faster. Well, now she had her answer—noticing anything about it at all would make it worse.

"About my driving."

"I would never," Cassia said.

"Oh really? How nice," Genevieve said, then turned to Cassia and leaned in with an exaggerated smile.

And winked.

Outside the car, the dotted yellow median line flashed by, providing a silent count in Cassia's head of the seconds going by while no one was watching where they were going.

Cassia broke first. "Look at the road, please! Okay, okay! Yes, you're going so fast you're scaring me."

Genevieve laughed, then relented and sat back in her seat and stared out the front windshield again. "Got ya."

"Not funny," Cassia muttered as she flexed her hand that had cramped around the handle on the ceiling.

"A little funny," Genevieve said.

"No, not even a little." Cassia slumped down in her seat. She tried to wrap her coat around herself even tighter. Now that the sun was down, the unusual warmth of the sunny day had evaporated into the crystal clear night above, leaving a distinct chill in the air. The stars were beautiful, though. She'd never seen anything like the Minnesota night sky in California.

"We're late," Genevieve said.

"Not that late. Besides, you're the one that insisted we go all the way back to your place for clothes." Cassia could feel those very clothes itching on her back as she spoke. Or maybe that was psychological.

"You're the one that didn't buy decent things to wear for a decade, forcing me to desperate actions."

"Not a decade," Cat said. She huffed and crossed her arms, and looked out the window.

"Those clothes were at least ten years old," Genevieve said as she slowed and turned the wheel to go on a side road that was even darker and more overgrown with trees than the main road.

"Good quality clothes from the thrift shop are timeless," Cassia said. "Are you sure you know where you're going?"

8

"Shortcut. Trust me."

Cassia's only answer was a snort.

But, amazingly enough, a few minutes later they emerged through a forest of trees high on a hill overlooking the back of a neighboring small town. The town's lights blazed. Every building along the main street was lit up, and cars packed the streets, jostling for parking spaces. Women of all ages packed the sidewalks and spilled out into the roads, making parking even harder for the drivers trying to navigate the streets. A few of the young ones even wore short dresses and high heels.

"Ho-wa," Genevieve said as they viewed the sight from the side road coming into town. "Apparently we are not the only ones excited about the grand opening."

Cassia slumped down even further into her seat. Great. Loads of witnesses to her humiliation.

CHAPTER 2

They found a parking spot a few streets over, just managing to pull in and get out of the way of the car behind them that was also cruising for a spot on the packed avenue. Light spilled over between the buildings on the main street, but the side street itself was unlit. As soon as Genevieve shut off the engine, the dark and quiet felt strangely disconnected from the hustle they'd passed through to get to it.

Stars twinkled down on them through the branches of the leafless trees of late autumn.

Laughter filtered through the night air to them. Mostly the higher tones of women.

"What exactly is this again?" Cassia asked.

Genevieve paused from her work of pulling the bare necessities of phone and wallet from her backpack and shoving them in her jacket to give Cassia a devilish smile. "Dance classes. Tonight is the grand opening."

Cassia gave her a dubious look. "Classes?"

"We don't have to pay—not tonight, anyway." Genevieve turned and shoved the backpack under a folded paper bag on the floor of the backseat, tucking it out of sight. She paused at Cassia's stare. "Oh, c'mon, it'll be fun. It's a *party.*"

"How come there are no men?" Cassia asked.

"Who said there are no men?" Genevieve asked, but didn't wait for an answer as she opened the door and got out of the car. The interior light blinded Cassia, then shut off again as Genevieve slammed the door shut.

Cassia got out of the car and followed.

"Why don't you leave your coat in the car?" Genevieve asked.

"You know why," Cassia said.

"You look great."

"I look…" Cassia didn't know how to finish the sentence, "…interesting."

"Same thing."

Cassia grunted.

They approached Main Street. Cassia had never been to this town before—Eugene, a sign said—but it looked very similar to Forgotten Valley, with the old-fashioned storefronts lined along a single major street. Several stores had taken advantage of the opening night party to stay open late. Polka music blasted out of a coffee shop and into the street, while a ladies' clothing store competed with country music. No one was backing down on the volume, each place trying to outblast the others. The light streamed through the plate glass window of the stores into the street, giving it a holiday feeling.

Genevieve practically glowed in the chaos.

"Okay. This does look like fun," Cassia said. So many people were out having a good time, and no one was staring at her outfit like she feared. They couldn't, actually, because she still had on her jacket. Small detail. "Let's get some cookies first."

"Good idea," Genevieve said. "Dinner was hours ago."

Two enormous peanut butter and chocolate cookies from

the coffee shop later, Cassia and Genevieve made their way down the street to the one large building that had banners of little triangle flags strung out to the trees in front of it.

The building was newer than the rest of the historical downtown and took up near a quarter of a block. People flowed in the front door from the street. A young girl of about twelve stood in front of the front door and rang a large bell. Cassia had a strange flashback to high school and the morning bells. She shook her head to rid herself of the feeling. This was supposed to be *fun*.

Cassia and Genevieve followed the crowd into the large room. The expansive room took up most of the building and looked even bigger with the light wood floors and the full wall mirror on the back wall. A ballet bar ran the length of the back wall.

"Wow, this looks like a real dance studio," Cassia said, impressed despite herself. This was not at all what she expected to find in a random small town in northern Minnesota.

"It really does," Genevieve said. "They must have spent a fortune on this place."

"What was it before?"

Genevieve shook her head. "Not this. I don't know what it was."

Most of the others in the place were women, with a few men scattered here and there, most looking like husbands who'd been dragged along and would have rather been at home watching a game, any game. That was all except for one perky fellow with a bright red hand-knit sweater and a smile to beat Genevieve's. His dark hair was slicked back in an odd way, but Cassia had the feeling he could be cute if someone gave him a wee bit of a makeover. Better yet, his smile said he was here for the party.

Now where were his friends?

Something seemed a little off here.

Cassia put her hands on her hips and turned to Genevieve. "Okay. We're here. I'm dressed up—very dressed up, thank you —so what is the surprise?"

"That," Genevieve said and pointed to a life-sized cutout of a man with a ridiculously square jaw, long, flowing dark hair, and no shirt. He stood on top of a rock and stared off into the distance as the sun glinted off his abs. He looked like he belonged on the cover of a romance novel.

A really cheesy romance novel.

Cassia slowly turned to Genevieve. "You're kidding, right?"

Genevieve winked at Cassia. "You know me, boy crazy all the way."

Cassia gaped. "That is not a boy."

"Very true."

"Genevieve!"

"Oh, stop. It's not like that," Genevieve said as she grabbed Cassia's arm and pulled her to the tables of food along the back wall. "This guy is a social marketing genius. When I found out he was coming here, I knew I had to check him out in person. Here," Genevieve said as she shoved a paper plate into Cassia's hands. "More sugar." She put an enormous rice crispy bar on the plate for Cassia and then pushed her down the line to fill the rest of the plate up on her own.

Much to Cassia's surprise, most of the goodies on the tables looked homemade and delicious. She decided to let herself be distracted by food. Genevieve looked around and gave little waves of greeting to women in the crowd. Cassia couldn't figure out if Genevieve knew them, or if she was just being friendly.

The crowd mingled and talked. A small group of women gathered in an admiring semicircle around the life-size cutout, with constant glances looking for the real thing to appear any moment.

Cassia finished her goodies, wiped the sugar off her hands,

and tossed her plate into the trash to go join Genevieve in the circle of women.

"So, what exactly happens tonight?" Cassia asked.

One woman looked at her with a happy smirk. "The ad said one-on-one lessons for every woman who shows up."

"For every *person* who shows up," the man in the red sweater corrected as he nudged into the circle. He, too, admired the cutout. "We could be here all night."

A happy sigh came from the group.

"You guys are silly. We could get dance lessons anywhere," Cassia said, trying to ignore how gorgeous the man looked in the picture. She was not going to act like a hormone crazed person. She was a scientist, after all. Or would be someday.

"But they wouldn't be lessons from Ricardo," a rich bass voice with a Greek accent said from behind Cassia.

From really close behind Cassia.

She turned quickly and nearly fell over into the wide chest of the in-person version of the man in the picture. He was much taller in the flesh and she found herself having to stare up into his eyes. His flowing hair was pulled back into the sexiest man bun she'd ever seen. Tight all black clothing covered him, from the tailored button-down shirt down to the trim pants that looked custom-made. She could feel the heat coming from his body.

He gave Cassia a little smile, and her traitorous heart pounded.

Scientist.

She was going to be a scientist.

Her heart couldn't care less. *Thump-thump-thump.*

Ricardo reached out and gently place his hands on her shoulders to take her jacket, asking with a raise of his eyebrows. Cassia nodded, her tongue feeling thick in her mouth.

He drew down her dowdy brown thrift shop coat and

tossed it to one side. A gasp came from the crowd, followed by a few titters.

Oh crap, she'd forgotten about her outfit.

Genevieve's custom outfit.

Cassia stood in the middle of the dance room along with Ricardo, now the center of everyone's attention, while wearing the shortest skirt she'd ever worn in her life. It was actually three layers of purple skirting layered to look like an upside down rose on her hips and not much more. At least Genevieve had let her wear black leggings, and a matching purple top was much more modest, almost looking like a kimono style wrap.

She looked like a manga cartoon character.

Behind Ricardo, Genevieve smiled at Cassia like a madwoman and gave two thumbs-up.

Cassia smiled back, then lifted her chin. If she was going to wear the crazy outfit she might as well flaunt it.

It helped that Ricardo's eyes never left hers. He didn't seem taken aback by her wild ensemble. He held out one hand and Cassia placed her hand in it. He nodded, and the fast waltz started pouring out of the speakers hung from the ceiling, then grabbed the small of her back with his other arm and swung her into motion. The other partygoers scampered back out of the way just in time as he swung her around and around, firmly guiding her with a hand on her back.

Despite Cassia's surety of being a klutz, he helped her find her footing through the dance and, for once, she actually felt graceful. Sexy even.

Unfortunately, it didn't take long before Cassia also felt dizzy and nauseous. She stumbled, squarely stepping on his foot with hers.

"Pick a spot on the wall," Ricardo said in his deep voice, its vibrations rumbling through his chest and into her very hands.

"Excuse me?"

"You're dizzy, right?" His Rs rolled as his breath tickled her ear.

"Yes. How did you know?" Cassia said, flustered.

"It's normal for beginners. They don't know to center themselves. Pick a spot on the wall and look at it until you can't anymore and then, when you turn, you bring your eyes back to it. It will keep your brain from getting too scrambled." He smiled down at her with deep brown eyes, nearly black. His voice had a strange quality of being understandable, but not loud enough for others to hear.

"Thank you," she said. She stared at a seam between the large panes of front window glass, carefully picking a spot high enough so she could avoid the eyes of the others watching. There was more than a little jealousy in some of their looks.

They danced for another minute in what felt like an eternity. Cassia reddened at the wealth of attention from Ricardo. She, of all people, had not been looking for it.

The others politely clapped when he finally let her go. She stumbled back into the crowd as the others rushed forward to be picked next.

———

Cassia and Genevieve stood at the back of the room by the food tables and watched as Ricardo twirled around partygoer after partygoer. Grandmas, young girls, and even the man in the red sweater. Some dancers took their turn and then snuck back into line, trying to get another go, while others staggered off, stunned at their experience with the gorgeous man.

"Did you really come here because of his social media skills?" Cassia asked as she nibbled on a pretzel.

"You betcha," Genevieve said. "This guy turned what should have been a two-minute career into twenty years in Hollywood. The dance studio is only his latest thing."

"What were the others?" Cassia asked.

"Novel cover model—"

"Of course."

Genevieve shot Cassia a look.

Cassia held up both her hands. "Please, go on. I won't interrupt, I promise," Cassia said.

"Yoga teacher, then yoga dynasty head leader..."

Cassia was dying to ask what a yoga dynasty was but bit her tongue to keep her word about not interrupting.

"... actor, he did a lot of commercials overseas, I guess. The thing is, he seems really good at getting people to talk about him. He makes it work for any business he tries, no matter how silly they seem at first. Look what he did here. Look at all these people," Genevieve said, motioning around the room.

"Are you sure it's not just because he's cute, even if he is a bit old?"

"He's not that old," Genevieve said as she chewed on a macaroon. "He started modeling pretty young."

"So why is he here?"

"I guess he wanted his daughter to spend some time with her grandfather. I had no idea the grandfather lived here."

"How'd you know all this stuff?" Cassia asked.

Genevieve smirked at her. "I told you, he's a genius at social media. He makes everyone feel like they're his friend. I bet that girl at the door was his daughter."

Genevieve and Cassia both looked over at the small table with a laptop computer hooked up to the room's speakers. The young girl from the door now wore enormous headphones and operated a sound system on the computer and watched for Ricardo's signals. She seemed a pro at it. There was never a break in the music.

Cassia turned to Genevieve. "I haven't seen you dancing with Ricardo."

"True. It's tempting, but I'm still trying to plan out the best way to approach him."

"For what?" Cassia asked.

"Mentorship. But you just can't come out and ask," Genevieve said as she reached for another homemade macaroon.

"Why not? He might just say yes."

"Maybe. But if I ask in front of everyone else, they'll think I'm hitting on him, and then they'll ask the same thing just so I don't get more attention."

Genevieve had a point. Everyone did want Ricardo's attention.

The strip of bells hung from the dance studio door jingled as it was flung open. A tall blonde woman in a trendy camel trench coat and high black riding boots strode into the dance studio. Energy radiated off her as she glared around the room. Her makeup was perfect, her eyebrows looked painted on. She stood in stark contrast to the more relaxed styles of the locals.

And if the sneer of her lip was anything, she didn't think much of the locals.

"For this, you drag my daughter across the country," she said to Ricardo. Her voice vibrated with anger.

For the first time that evening since he entered the studio, Ricardo stopped moving and released his dance partner, who backed away, leaving him and the woman in the center of the room.

Ricardo's face was expressionless, the easy smile he'd had all evening gone.

CHAPTER 3

Everyone stood at rapt attention to the sharp blonde woman glaring at Ricardo. She was nearly as tall as he was. It was almost like watching two titans face off before a fight. And she looked ready for a fight.

Cassia felt dizzy, realizing she'd been holding her breath. The creak of floorboards under someone shifting their weight echoed through the studio, but there were no other sounds.

Red creeped over Ricardo's face. He gave a wan smile.

"Welcome, Polina. Would you like a free lesson?" he asked politely.

"Of course I don't want a free lesson, you lumbering hulk of…" With some effort, the woman stopped herself from completing the sentence.

"I'm very sorry you are upset. Perhaps we can go out back and have a discussion?" Ricardo asked. He held out a hand, but Polina just sniffed.

"My daughter. I would like to see my daughter," she said.

"Your *stepdaughter* is here," Ricardo said, motioning to the girl at the sound system. He emphasized the word stepdaughter clearly so everyone in the room could hear it.

Polina turned toward the girl and opened her arms. "Come here, baby."

Everyone turned to look at the girl. The girl edged further behind the table and gave a minute shake of her head.

"Honey," Polina said, an edge in her voice.

The girl shook her head again.

Polina took a step toward the sound table. At the same time, Ricardo stepped in between Polina and the girl.

"Perhaps we can discuss this later. Jane is busy," he said.

"Jane should show respect to her elders," Polina said. The crowd muttered. While no one could argue with her words, no one was a fan of the woman's attitude and overbearing behavior toward the young girl. Several mothers in their best dresses edged toward the girl, forming a small crescent of protection.

Polina stopped in her tracks, unwilling to push forward into the group of protectors. She turned back to Ricardo. "Yes, perhaps you're right. Here is not the place. These gawkers have no business in our family affairs." Contempt dripped from her voice.

Ricardo's jaw clenched, but all he did was give her a curt nod. "Thank you, Polina." The crowd gave way like the Red Sea as he walked toward the door and held it open for the blonde woman. She hesitated, then walked briskly to the door and out it without another word.

Ricardo let the door fall shut. Someone giggled nervously in the studio and then everyone broke out in conversation at once.

"Well, that was interesting," Genevieve said to Cassia in a low whisper.

Genevieve's car rolled through the night as fast as they dared. Fog had rolled in, making the passage through the deer filled woods even more hazardous. Genevieve even kept the music down low, giving Cassia a welcome reprieve from sound after the hours of loud dance music at the studio.

Ricardo had tried to bring up the mood again after Polina left, but the spell had been broken. People cheered up a bit, though, when he promised a full week of free lessons for everyone who'd come to the opening night party. Even Cassia had been willing to sign up for that. Maybe that reward money would come in by the time he started asking for real money. Cassia had only been in town for a month, but she was already going stir crazy in that mansion all by herself, and she didn't want her only social time to be when she was at the diner working.

"I can't believe after all that you never danced with him, not even once," Cassia said, giving Genevieve an elbow.

"Hey, I'm driving! Don't distract the driver," Genevieve said with mock outrage.

"Since when are you that careful?" Cassia said with a tease.

"Since I'm poor and can't afford another car if I crash this one. You might think I'm all fun and games, young lady, but I take these things very seriously." Genevieve's serious face lasted for exactly three seconds before she busted up laughing.

"That lady was sort of crazy," Cassia said. At least no one had commented on Cassia's outfit after the incident.

"She must've flown right in from LA. No one around here looks like that," Genevieve said.

Cassia shot her a look.

"Yes, I would know. I'm used to being the odd man out. Woman. You know what I mean."

"I do," Cassia said. She picked at a loose thread on her tights. The excitement of the night was wearing off, and her eyes were drooping. Tomorrow was a long day at the diner.

Sunday brunch. Almost a town holiday, the way everyone acted. It seemed everyone came to the diner on Sundays.

"Hey, you're not getting out of it that easy," Cassia said. "If you want him to mentor you, you need to ask him."

"Yeah, you're right," Genevieve said. "Didn't seem like good timing after that scene, though."

"Good point. You can hit him up in class."

Genevieve brightened. "Yeah, hopefully the weekday classes won't be too busy."

"Hopefully," Cassia said, but she wasn't counting on it. The impromptu sign-up sheets Ricardo had brought out had been pretty full by the time they had left.

They made the rest of the journey to the Mandress mansion in silence. The fog cleared a bit as they got out of the woods and the land climbed the slow gentle hills up to the mansion's property.

Cassia admired the huge structure under the moonlight. Three stories and two wings. Large enough to be a small apartment building in any normal city, but if she could live there for one full year and satisfy the conditions of her aunt's will, it would be all hers, along with a goodly sum of money that her lawyer still hadn't been able to get the exact figure of. But it should be enough.

Enough money.

A phrase Cassia never thought would ever apply to her.

She just had to make it until the lawyer could unravel the financial mess made by the fraudulent housekeeper, aka thief, or until the reward money came through. Whichever came first.

Genevieve pulled around the gentle turnabout in the front of the mansion, originally meant for horse carriages, making a point to pull around counterclockwise so Cassia's passenger door opened directly to the front door of the mansion.

"Do you want me to come in?" Genevieve asked.

Cassia shook her head. "I think I'm safe. Thanks for asking,"

"Always do," Genevieve said. She watched as Cassia grabbed her bag from the backseat and then made her way through the front door, only struggling a bit with the lock.

———

Inside, Cassia threw her bag of clothes on a chair in the entryway and flicked on the lights. From the outside, the mansion looked all 18th-century old-school dark doom and gloom, but inside, at least on the first floor, it was newly remodeled and light and airy. Light blonde hardwood graced the floor, with pastel greens and blues on the walls. Yellow and cream French furniture dotted the rooms, just enough to have some place to sit, but not so much as to make the vast space feel crowded.

It was all very beautiful and posh. Cassia found it a little intimidating. No matter what bad qualities the old housekeeper Sarah may have had, having poor taste was not one of them.

Miss Mansfield, her inherited black cat with beautiful gold eyes, sat waiting in one of the entryway chairs. Cassia had no idea how she did it, but Miss Mansfield was always waiting for her when she got in the front door. Perhaps she heard cars coming up the drive. In any case, having only lived in the mansion for a month, it already felt only proper to see Miss Mansfield first thing when she opened the door.

"Hungry?" Cassia asked. It was past midnight, but Cassia always gave Miss Mansfield another meal whenever she came home, no matter how many times she'd already been fed before.

Miss Mansfield gave a delicate little meow and arched her back, then led the way back toward the kitchen at the back of the house. Cassia followed, flicking on the hallway lights, and then the kitchen lights as she went. The kitchen—a white monstrosity of architect's digest meets farm kitchen—could have held her entire old apartment in California. Much to Cassia's delight, this one held mostly food, including what seemed like a year's worth of food for Miss Mansfield, and a pantry's worth of nearly that for her. The fridge and freezer were running a little low, and she was counting on her lawyer, Nate Perauski, to get her some funds before the situation became dire.

She didn't even want to ask what the property taxes were on the mansion. Those alone were probably more than her entire rent in California. That was definitely not something she could pay with a waitress's salary.

Cassia selected a can of fresh cat food for Miss Mansfield and laid it out on a clean plate, then made a cup of tea for herself. Cradling the hot mug, she walked back down the hallway to the enormous two-story library of the mansion and flicked on the light.

The library was packed floor-to-ceiling with books on custom shelves that ran the length of the room on two sides, many of the books rare editions on her favorite topic, astronomy. She looked at them longingly. Soon, she could stop working at the diner and have more time to spend digging through this library. Not only was she interested in the books, but she was hoping to find another note from her aunt, Mildred Mandress, tucked between the pages. She knew so little about the enigmatic woman who'd left her this sprawling property, and everywhere she tried to get more information it seemed to be one dead end after another.

———

Brilliant morning sunshine poured into Cassia's bedroom. She'd done a poor job of pulling the curtains shut the previous night and now the sun woke her hours before she wanted to get up. Cassia groaned and then threw an arm over her eyes. After a moment, she flopped around from side to side in frustration. It was no use. She was awake now, and wasn't going to be able to fall back asleep.

Stupid sun.

Cassia threw back the Matelasse cover and swung her legs over the edge of the bed. Between the enormous four-poster walnut bed and the stacks of boxes, there was little room in the bedroom to walk. She was going to have to fix that one of these days.

But not today.

Genevieve usually picked her up on Sundays so she wouldn't have to bike back home exhausted. One of these days, and soon, she would have a late model car to drive, but like all things bureaucratic, that too was still being tied up with trying to figure out what Sarah, the old housekeeper, had done with the title. In the meanwhile, the car sat in the garage along with three other very nice cars that Cassia also couldn't use.

Cassia padded her way into the kitchen in her oversized men's pajamas and fumbled with the coffee maker, pulling a clean mug from the dishwasher. She still wasn't over the thrill of having freshly washed dishes that she didn't have to do herself. Between the coffee, the bright sunny morning, and the beautiful house, things were feeling pretty good.

Miss Mansfield came into the kitchen from wherever she'd been hiding.

"Good morning, sunshine. Would you like some breakfast?" Cassia asked.

Miss Mansfield answered with a polite meow and Cassia fixed her breakfast.

Cassia opened the back door of the kitchen, letting in the cool morning breeze. The yard was still a mess, with weeds everywhere and an overgrown path, but that too would have to wait. She would probably have enough cash to actually hire someone to do the yard work, another thought that thrilled her.

But first, she had to get through the next few weeks and make some money.

Much sooner than she wanted, pounding came from the front door. Cassia glanced at the huge clock on the wall and yelped when she realized how late it was. "Coming," she called as she gulped the last of her coffee and put the cup in the sink, and then scurried to the front door.

She pulled open the door. Genevieve stood on the stoop, her arms crossed and her hip cocked. She wore her light blue waitress uniform over her normal combat boots. Her dark hair was styled as usual in a wild asymmetrical manga style. With the light streaming in behind her, she looked like some kind of strange 1950s superhero.

"Still in your pajamas?" Genevieve asked.

"Um, sorry," Cassia said.

Genevieve waved away her apology. "I was counting on it. I know how slow you are in the morning." Genevieve pushed Cassia toward her bedroom to change and then clomped off to the kitchen to raid the fridge. It had become something of a tradition. Genevieve claimed food found in other people's refrigerators tasted better than anything you had in your own. Which Cassia found sort of funny, considering some of it Genevieve had stocked herself since Cassia did not have a car.

Cassia pulled on her waitress uniform in record time and pulled back her hair into a boring ponytail. She didn't have the wild style that Genevieve did, but at least it would stay out of her eyes.

Genevieve was petting Miss Mansfield and rubbing noses with the black kitty when Cassia finally made it back into the kitchen and they could go to work.

Once Cassia locked the back door and they made their way

out the front door, which she locked as well, Genevieve stood by the driver's door of her car, waiting with a strange smile on her face as Cassia came around to open the passenger door.

"What?" Cassia asked, instantly suspicious.

"I brought a surprise for you. This is as long as I could wait," Genevieve said.

Cassia looked around but didn't see anything unusual.

"It's on the passenger seat," Genevieve said. She pulled open the driver's door and got in.

Opening the passenger door, Cassia looked inside. The only thing on the seat was a folded Forgotten Valley Sunday newspaper, headlines side down. She grabbed it and pulled it out. On the front, just above the fold, an enormous picture of Polina that took two thirds of the paper, under the headline *Hollywood Film Production Begins.*

Cassia scanned the article until Genevieve leaned her head over to the passenger side and spoke.

"She's a real-life movie producer. How cool is that?"

How odd is that? Cassia thought. The woman certainly didn't seem to like it here. Why would she bring an entire movie production to this state?

CHAPTER 4

The inside of the diner was chaos. People of all ages filled every chair, and some chairs even had two occupants, one stacked on top of another. None of the customers seemed to mind. They were busy talking to each other, smiling and laughing. But for Cassia, the crush of people just made her job that much harder. She had to weave through the tables with plates of hot food and not spill on anyone. Give her a calculation of how quickly the moon was receding from the Earth due to tidal drag and she could knock that out of the park down to the exact number of inches per year, but talking to this many people in a loud environment, and having to remember all their orders? Forget it.

She glanced down at her green pad and grimaced. It was a scribble of notes, trying to write down each thing down so she would not forget.

And then she still forgot.

Luckily, the customers of Smith's Diner and Deli were generally forgiving. And even more luckily for them, Genevieve did her best to help Cassia out.

The morning rush had come and gone, but even so, there was still a line out the door at 3 pm.

"Where are all these people coming from?" Cassia asked. She wiped her brow with the back of her hand. In a rush to pour waters for a table of six, she had gotten ice cold water all over her hands and down the front of her blue dress. Although it looked terrible, it was refreshingly cool. Maybe people would tip her more out of pity.

"Everyone's trying to enjoy the last of the nice weather," Genevieve said as she swooped behind the counter and gracefully deposited a full stack of dishes in the bus bin. "How you doing?"

"Not well," Cassia said. "This waitressing is hard. Every time I remember something and do it right, I seem to forget something else and end up doing it wrong." Cassia had been putting a good face on it, but a few hours of performing so poorly was starting to wear on her.

Genevieve laughed. Cassia whirled to glare at her.

Holding her hands up, Genevieve backed up. "I'm sorry. It's just so cute the way you've apologized to almost every table."

"That's not cute!" Cassia said, realizing how petulant she sounded even as the words came out. When Cassia thought of cute, she thought of something like a perfectly pristine white teacup poodle barking a chipper little pristine bark. No, she was not cute.

"I'm sorry, I'm sorry," Genevieve said, managing to push down her laughter.

The bells on the door rang as a large family came in wearing flannels of all colors, if all colors were green, red, and blue intermixed with black. Cassia groaned. She couldn't even remember the drink orders for two people, she'd never survive eight at one table.

Leaning into Cassia, Genevieve asked, "Will you forgive me if I take that group?"

Crossing her arms, Cassia frowned and then said quietly, "Yes."

"Done and done," Genevieve said as she walked back out from behind the counter and grabbed a stack of menus on her way to greet the group.

Following on the heels of the family, another person entered the diner. He was so tall, Cassia could meet his eyes over the heads of the family. With his dark hair slicked back, and his massive body, there was only one person that could be —Nate Perauski, her lawyer. No one else in Forgotten Valley was even close to his size.

Cassia checked her tables and the window to the back grill, and decided she had a second to go talk to the man.

"Hey, Nate, how are you?" Cassia asked as she came over with a menu after the family went by.

"I'm good, Miss Lemon. I don't need that. You know the drill—"

"Chef's special," Cassia said with a laugh.

"Of course. The counter is fine."

Cassia nodded up at him, astounded as always at his huge size. Luckily, two stools just opened up at the end of the Formica unit, giving the man a little extra room to spread out.

"Coffee?" Cassia asked, ready to walk off and get it.

"Yes, but I'm actually here to see you more than anything else."

"On a Sunday?" Cassia asked. Nate had a law office in town that they usually met at for official business.

"I've lucked out with jury duty on Monday and figured you might want the news as soon as possible, and not possibly after two weeks, or worse."

"News?" Cassia asked, stopping in her tracks and all thoughts of coffee gone.

30

"Plus, I wanted to tell you in person," he said with a smile, enjoying the look of hope on her face. "We got a letter late Friday. We've found some of your aunt's main bank accounts, including the one mentioned for you for the probationary period. As soon as we get some documentation over to them, you should have access. I spent a good chunk of Saturday seeing how far I could get that prepared."

"You don't normally work on Saturdays, do you?" Cassia asked, surprised.

"Well, you know how Mrs. Anderson feels about computers," Nate said. He was remarkably understanding about his secretary who only liked to work on electric typewriters, and had her own avocado green IBM model she'd brought in herself that she insisted on using and nothing else. That typewriter must have been at least forty years old. It, Mrs. Anderson, and her spectacular blond beehive hairdo were all one of a kind. At Cassia's look, Nate went on. "She does answer the phone, and keeps me from being too lonely in that little office."

Yeah, there was value in that. Being lonely sucks.

But money! Soon Cassia was going to have some! Suddenly everything in the diner looked bright and shiny and new. She wanted to do a little dance.

Then a new thought came, and a frown crossed Cassia's face. "Enough for the mansion bills too?" she asked, lowering her voice as a woman seated at a table next to them not so subtly leaned in to hear more of Cassia's and Nate's conversation.

Nate shook his head. "That is not a worry. Your aunt was quite the manager. She even had the utilities and taxes on autopay. A marvel, I must say."

"Wow," Cassia mouthed.

Just past Nate, a customer waved to get Cassia's attention. She nodded at him, then said to Nate, "I'll get your coffee and be right back."

Time to get her customers their food so she could get her butt back to Nate and find out how she was getting some cash from the estate.

———

Two hours later, Cassia waved goodbye to a few customers as they exited the diner and walked down the street past the plate glass windows. The rest of the diner was quiet, and most of the tables stood empty as the last of the Sunday rush trailed off. With Genevieve's help, Cassia had managed to get some time to talk to Nate while also delivering food to her tables and keeping up with her half of the bussing of the dishes. Now her feet ached, and she sat gratefully on a stool at the counter with a sigh. Genevieve brought over two cups of cocoa and sat next to Cassia, sliding one cup over to her.

The only customer left in the diner was Mrs. Jenson sitting in one of the window booths. She was a Sunday fixture, and would happily yell if she needed anything, but for now she sat in the booth and knitted a bright electric blue scarf, as if the diner was a second living room for her. In a way, it was. She was here every Sunday. After her husband had passed several years ago, she decided she would never ever make another Sunday dinner again and instead spent Sundays in the diner. This week, Mrs. Jenson's hair was dyed an electric blue that matched the scarf she was working on. In the short month Cassia had been in Forgotten Valley, she'd seen three colors on Mrs. Jenson's head, but Genevieve assured her that it had been nearly every color of the rainbow. Mrs. Jenson was one of Genevieve's favorite customers, and Cassia could see why. They were like mother and daughter, in a very hands-off sort of way.

Genevieve leaned in and touched her shoulder to Cassia's. "So, what's the scoop?" Genevieve asked. "I saw that twinkle in your eye after talking to Nate."

Cassia looked down and smiled despite her exhaustion. She took a sip of the hot cocoa. The marshmallows had just started to melt, lending an extra bit of sweetness to the hot drink.

"Whatever could you be talking about?" Cassia asked, affecting mock ignorance. She refused to meet Genevieve's increasingly aggravated gaze.

"Stop that," Genevieve said, giving Cassia's stool a light kick. When Cassia didn't answer, Genevieve turned back to the counter and sipped her own drink, then said with her own fake tone, "Now that I think about it, I might be a little light on gas. You wouldn't mind walking home, would you?"

Cassia dropped all pretense of nonchalance and stared at Genevieve with her mouth hanging open.

Genevieve busted out laughing. "It's not that far."

"It is too that far. Stop threatening me," Cassia said. She lived twenty miles outside of town if she was willing to go through muddy fields, further if she insisted on the luxury of a road. There was no way she was walking home.

"All right, all right. You know I'm just kidding," Genevieve said.

"And you know that's not funny," Cassia said, giving Genevieve a little glare before settling down to drink more hot cocoa. She was too tired for more verbal sparring.

Genevieve said nothing, waiting patiently. Only the click of Mrs. Jensen's knitting needles echoed in the diner. Some time during the afternoon, the music had gotten turned down and then forgotten about. Cassia appreciated the quiet.

"It sounds like I'm finally getting some money, and soon. Like, real money," Cassia finally said.

"Real money?" Genevieve asked. "Pay the bills money, or splurge on diamonds money?" She looked more excited than Cassia felt. Not a trace of jealousy on her face.

Cassia shrugged. She didn't know. Besides, any money would be a welcome change.

"When?"

"Maybe this week," Cassia said. "Nate's going to text me when he finds out for sure. He's got jury duty this week."

"Whoo-hoo, jury duty, how exciting," Genevieve said, not a trace of sarcasm in her voice. "I almost had jury duty once, but they turned me away because they thought I looked too weird. Next time, I'm going to have my special jury duty outfit ready to go. It will be all brown, like my hair will be. Totally normal."

Cassia doubted that was even possible. Even in all brown, Genevieve would find a way to stand out, something the woman seemed completely ignorant of. She looked earnest about getting in to do jury duty.

"You're serious, are you?" Cassia asked.

"Heck yeah. Jury duty seems like the best. You get to hear all this gossipy stuff, and find out about people's lives, without being the one in trouble."

That was a good point. It was a good real-life soap opera. Cassia shook her head. Her one and only experience with jury duty had involved a lot of driving in Los Angeles and sitting in a waiting room, only to be dismissed after three days. It had been the opposite of exciting, or even gossipy. All she'd thought about was all the lectures she was missing. Maybe she'd had the wrong attitude.

...Nah.

Genevieve whipped her Honda around the driveway and pulled to a stop in front of Cassia's door. The sun was just setting, setting the whole mansion in a beautiful relief of pinks and oranges that also reflected from all the windows.

It would look great as soon as she had the money to get the outside fixed and the horrible dark blue paint job replaced with something better.

34

Genevieve turned off the engine and got out of the driver's seat as Cassia got her bags together and exited the passenger door. Genevieve pulled a large aluminum foil pan out of the backseat and slid it onto the front stoop for Cassia. Trent had sent Cassia home with the leftover casserole from the diner. It worked out well—she got the leftovers so Trent didn't have to throw them in the garbage, and she was willing to accept less cash as part of the deal. Cassia appreciated not having to shop or cook for a few more days.

"You sure you don't want to come and spy on some of the fancy movie filming with me? Who knows who we might see," Genevieve asked.

"You don't even know for sure it's going to be there," Cassia said, pointing out that Genevieve's information was only hearsay. One of the diners had told Genevieve in confidence that a permit had been pulled in the nearby town for the next day. Cassia just thought that the guy wanted a date, something that Genevieve vehemently denied.

"It might be there. Definitely an exciting possibility since we don't have to work tomorrow," Genevieve said.

"No thanks, I'm going to spend my day off exploring the mansion, something I should've done weeks ago."

"We did explore it," Genevieve said.

"That was in a rush to make sure I didn't go to jail for murder. This is different. It'll be nice and slow, and I'll see if I can learn more about my aunt."

Genevieve waved that off. "The learning about your aunt part is cool, but the rest sounds pretty boring."

Cassia shrugged.

"Just make sure you have a new outfit for Tuesday if you don't want me dressing you again," Genevieve said, her wicked smile giving away her preference. "Tuesday is our first formal dance lessons with the man himself. I'm going to bring something just in case you don't pass my inspection." Genevieve stood with her hands on her hips until Cassia nodded agreement, then hopped into her car and turned over the engine.

Cassia waved as Genevieve drove away. She had no doubt Genevieve would make good on her threat. Cassia pressed her lips together into a thin line; she was not going to wear another Genevieve outfit again if it was the last thing she did.

CHAPTER 5

The weak light of a threatening day filtered into the tall windows at the end of the long library room of the Mandress mansion. Despite the outer foreboding appearance of the place, the inside—at least the first floor—was newly redecorated in light and airy colors.

Birch wood shelving filled the two-story-high wall ahead of Cassia, jam-packed with books of all shapes and sizes, many ancient with hand-tooled leather covers, and others much newer, with pictures of gravity wells on the covers, or star clusters, or galaxies. This room was the promised land of any scientist interested in astronomy or physics. Another matching wall stood behind her. Only the end walls had no books—the far end was filled with windows overlooking the estate, while the doorway wall had old drawings of landscapes hung over several comfortable armchairs.

Cassia sat at one of the long tables in the middle of the long room, sipping her coffee and trying to come up with a plan.

Her only clue from her aunt about what had been going on in the house before her aunt had died had come in the form of a note inside a book. So, it made sense to check all the books for notes. They were the only personal things still left in the house, for now.

The problem was there were a lot of them.

A lot, lot of them.

The room could have been the entire library of a small town.

Going through those books looking for another note would take a long time. Not to mention a lot of ladder climbing. The top shelves were only accessible by the wood ladders on rails that ran along each wall. They looked like more fun than they were, as Cassia had discovered the first time she climbed one to see what a red volume was (an ancient primer on Newtonian physics) and nearly fell when she realized how high up she was.

If she slipped off a ladder and injured herself while no one else was in the mansion, it could be really bad. The place was way further out in the country than yelling distance for help. Cassia patted her pocket to make sure her cell phone was there.

On the plus side, going through the library would not be entirely unpleasant. Astronomy was her passion, and she was determined to be a professional astronomer, if she could get through this year in the house first.

The house she'd inherited from an aunt she'd never known existed until she got the letter from the lawyers.

The house that also had a telescope attached.

How many houses could say that?

The telescope was an ancient relic, but still, it had its own fancy dome, and it was all hers. In other words, the whole situation was like someone had dug around in Cassia's mind, pulled out her wildest fantasy, and decided to make it a reality.

Cassia shook her head and turned to stare out windows to the gray weather outside. It looked like the storm promised over the morning news would arrive by noon. At least she hadn't planned on doing anything outside on her day off.

Miss Mansfield gave a little meow at Cassia's look. She sat on the same table Cassia was at, delicately licking her paws and cleaning her face after her breakfast in the kitchen. Her black fur and golden eyes gleamed with health, even in the low light. Miss Mansfield was nice company, as long as Cassia got her name right. If not, Miss Mansfield had a penchant for stepping on toes, which was surprisingly painful for an animal the size of a loaf of bread. Cassia had never had a cat before, and it was harder than it looked on TV. Miss Mansfield was not shy about letting her preferences be known.

Cassia gave Miss Mansfield a pet and was rewarded with an arched back and a purr.

Standing, Cassia set down her coffee on the table and went to grab the ladder for the wall in front of her.

She might as well get started checking the books.

———

Several hours and much dust later, Cassia replaced a book on the bottom shelf, then coughed into her sleeve. As tempting as it had been to put each book on the table or floor when done checking them for notes, she'd forced herself to replace them back on the shelves. There were too many books to not put them back. It wouldn't take long for there to not be enough room to stand if she hadn't.

Flipping through each book as fast as she could before going on had only gotten her through one quarter of one wall. That was only an eighth of the total. This was not her idea of a fun day off.

Not finding anything in all that time made her feel even worse.

She glanced outside. Sometime during the morning, the

dark clouds had blown away. It actually looked nice and sunny outside.

"Meow," Miss Mansfield said before stretching and then walking off and out the door. Cassia watched enviously.

"Good idea," Cassia said to herself. "Just one more for good luck." She turned and looked at the bookshelf and picked a purple volume in the middle of the wall at random and pulled it out. A beautiful photograph of a nebula graced the cover. It looked newer than most of the books on the shelf.

Cassia flipped it open and fanned the pages, only halfheartedly paying attention when an old yellowed black-and-white photograph slipped out and felt to the floor. She gasped, then put the book on the table and scrambled to pick up the picture. It was of an older man bundled in a fur hat and coat, shaking the hand of Senior Mandress, her grandfather and the builder of the mansion, as well as a huge astronomy enthusiast. Cassia recognized her grandfather from a photograph Nate, her lawyer, had dug up for her.

But who was the man whose hand he was shaking? Cassia peered closer at the photograph. In the background, several photographers stood, wearing trench coats and carrying huge cameras with old-fashioned flashes perched on top. It looked like a paparazzi shoot from an old movie. Whoever that man was, he was really important.

She flipped over the photograph. A single line written in blue ink said *V.P.N., 1957.*

VPN? They didn't even have the internet in 1957, much less VPNs, Cassia thought nonsensically. She quickly realized her mistake. There were periods after each letter. It must be the initials for someone's name. She flipped the photo over again to stare at their faces. The man looked very familiar.

Near the top of the image, a dome glinted, and to one side of the row of photographers, a green-shaded desk lamp stood on a dark worktable.

Cassia gasped. That photo was taken in the telescope dome room of this house!

Cassia sat at the island of the mansion kitchen, chewing on a pimento loaf and mustard sandwich. Genevieve had gotten her addicted to the things, and now it was her daily salt fix. On the counter in front of her lay the photograph of her grandfather and the strange man, as well as her phone, open to the contact for Smith, Chase and Jones law firm in New York.

Having had some success in finding a new clue about the house, Cassia thought about tackling her other big project: trying to find out why she'd been left the phone number for the law firm, taped under a chair like something right out of a spy novel.

Sucking in a big breath of air to brace herself, Cassia picked up her phone and pressed the green call button.

The phone rang in the old-fashioned ring tone as usual, something Cassia was starting to hate, followed by the tinny voice of a young man. "Smith, Chase, and Jones. How may I direct your call?"

"It's me," Cassia said.

The man sighed on the other end of the line. "Miss—"

"Lemon," Cassia supplied.

"Miss Lemon, I did tell you the first dozen times you called that we would call you back when we knew more—"

"I didn't call a dozen times," Cassia said, indignant. She'd only called nine times. If he was going to go all snarky on her, at least he could get his facts straight.

"—and then and only then we will call you back to discuss any relevant issues," he said, continuing as if she had not spoken. "The partner in charge of all communications for inci-dences such as these is on vacation."

Incidences?

"You've been telling me the same thing for a month," Cassia said.

The young man did not say anything. Cassia did not like the implied answer that she was dense.

"Are you telling me someone has been on vacation for a month?" Cassia asked, finally.

"I believe I have been telling you that," the young man said with an overly polite tone.

She'd never wanted to kick anyone in the shins so much in her life. Not a mature response, Cassia, she thought to herself, then forced herself to take a deep breath.

"Is this how you treat all your clients?" Cassia asked instead.

"Are you a client?" he asked.

Was she a client?

All she had was a note with the phone number of the law firm and a series of numbers that the young man claimed meant nothing. It hadn't meant exactly nothing, Cassia had discovered, realizing that the numbers were actually the speed of light as written in meters per second, but the numbers themselves had gotten her nowhere with the law firm.

Cassia clenched her free hand as she thought. That number had been from her aunt.

"I'm sure my aunt or grandfather was, and they gave me this number, which meant they intended to include me too," Cassia said.

"Do you have a will or other document stating as such?" the young man asked. His singsong tone mocked Cassia. It was not the first time he asked her that very question, and they both knew it.

Cassia didn't bother to say no, and instead just growled into the phone.

"Have a great day, Miss," he said, then hung up. Cassia

could just hear the smarmy smile in his voice. She clicked the end button on her phone hard, even though he had already disconnected the line.

Stupid New York lawyers.

———

Shifting her weight from foot to foot, Cassia looked around Smith's Deli and Diner while trying to get some blood back into her feet. Her old shoes were just that, old. There was not enough padding left in the rubber to last a full shift in the diner. Or at least the six hours she'd been there, and she had more time on her feet coming with their dance lessons that night.

The midafternoon lull in business left the diner a quiet place. Tourist season was over, and few locals came in between lunch and dinner. All that was left was the final prep for the next shift coming in at four thirty—a shift she'd not be around for, thank you very much.

She looked around. Not a single customer was still in the diner and Genevieve was in back helping Trent. What would it hurt if she sat down for five minutes to rest her feet? Just as she was about to slide into one of the front booths, she happened to glance up and see Sheriff Andrews standing outside in front of the diner. He stood with his hands on his hips, glaring at her bike which was locked to a meter. Slowly, he moved his hands from his hips and pulled out a large ticket pad from his right rear pocket. It was impressive he could even fit it in there considering how tight the pants were.

"No. No, no, no…" Cassia said, her thoughts of a rest abandoned as she rushed out the door of the diner, sending the door's bells jingling.

She ran to the meter, trying to block Sheriff Andrew's view of her bike.

"It's just a bike," she said. "Don't give me a ticket. It's

locked. It has a license," Cassia said, instantly regretting mentioning the license. It was a California license. Who knew what rule Sheriff Andrews had about bike licenses in Forgotten Valley. He had rules about everything, and she didn't understand most of them.

"You can't lock your bike to a meter. It interferes with the normal business of using the meter," Sheriff Andrew said. As always, Cassia was distracted by his deep blue eyes. She wondered if he practiced hypnotizing people with them, or if it was just an accident caused by how intense they were.

He also smelled really good. Sort of lemony, and minty, and clean. It was a weird combination, but good, and also very distracting.

"Miss Lemon," Sheriff Andrews said when Cassia didn't answer, "parking your bike here is a serious offense."

Cassia stared at him, then checked the street. There were only two cars parked on the entire street, and none even close to where her bike was. "No one was trying to use the meter. It didn't cause any harm."

Sheriff Andrews looked unimpressed. "That's irrelevant. Someone *might* have tried to use the meter, and couldn't. Or worse yet, tried to use it, and then injured themselves by falling and breaking a leg and then suing the city because the equipment was not in working order because *someone* blocked it in an irresponsible way, putting us all in legal jeopardy." He breathed heavily after getting all those words out.

Cassia blinked. In a small voice, she said, "No one tried to use it."

"How do you know? Were you out here the whole time the bike was locked to the meter? I didn't see you when I came up."

"No, not out here, right here," Cassia said. She pointed to the diner. "I was in there all day. I would've known that there was a problem."

"Inside there is not the same thing as being outside here," Sheriff Andrews said, pointing to the ground in front of the meter. He recrossed his arms and looked down at Cassia.

A frown crept over her face. She couldn't see a way out of this. No matter what she said, it would be wrong. "Why are you giving me such a hard time?"

A strange expression flitted over his face, one that could almost have been embarrassment, but it was gone so quickly she couldn't be sure she'd actually seen it. He shifted on his feet and spoke gruffly. "I'm not giving you a hard time. I just want everyone in this town to be safe and secure and have things go the way they're supposed to. I guess you big-city folk don't understand how that works. I'll let it go this time, but don't park your bike here again. Tell your boss," he motioned to the diner, "to give you a spot inside for it."

Shoving the parking pad back in his right rear pocket, he stalked off. Cassia stared longer than she should have as he walked away, then ran back inside once he turned the corner.

———

"Okay, girl, let's see what you got," Genevieve said. She stubbornly sat at one of the booths in the diner even though their shift was over and they were supposed to get going. "I'm not going anywhere until I see you in a decent outfit."

Cassia held her backpack that she'd lugged from the mansion that morning. It had been a bike-to-work sort of day since Genevieve had had to give Roger a ride somewhere at the last minute due to some sort of emergency. Roger was the town handyman. He was actually the only handyman for several towns in any direction. Even Trent was okay with Cassia being a little late in the interest of keeping Roger happy. Commercial grade freezers and refrigerators were hard to fix, and even more expensive to replace.

Squeezing her backpack, Cassia regretted both bringing its contents, and not having the foresight to also bring a hanger and hang up said contents when she got to work that morning. What she regretted most of all was the thought of facing Genevieve wearing what she had brought.

"How bad can it be?" Genevieve said as she worried at a strand of her blue hair. Even after a long day of waiting tables, she still looked as put together as ever. She had changed immediately from her waitressing outfit to a cute silver dress for dancing even as Cassia had dragged her feet.

"Can't I just wear a shirt and pants?" Cassia asked. She'd packed those, too, just in case.

"Is it an amazing shirt and pants?" Genevieve asked.

"Just... jeans," Cassia said.

"I've seen your jeans. Come on, let's have some fun, do something different. It's not like you'll ever see these people again. Probably. I mean, it's a whole other town away."

True. Even if it was full of people from this town, Cassia should not care so much. What was the worst that could happen? She would just look silly.

Ten minutes later, Cassia emerged from the diner bathroom, walking gingerly on the unfamiliar heels and feeling the skirt swish around her legs. Luckily, the dress was mostly polyester and didn't have a wrinkle on it, even after being crammed in her backpack all day. Despite that unlikely pedigree, it looked amazing—a long silhouette of red material with a subtle flare in the skirt and the barest hint of a slit. She'd even tried to put her hair up with hairpins she'd found at the bottom of a moving box and had forgotten about entirely.

"Holy cow, you look like something right out of a tango movie!" Genevieve said as she got up to check Cassia out. "Where did you get this and why didn't we find it the other day?"

"It was in a box of my school stuff. It's a costume from a

high school play. They let us keep them when the school closed…" Cassia said, trailing off as she tried to back away from Genevieve's examination of the material.

"Were you any good in the play?" Genevieve asked distractedly.

"No, not really," Cassia said. It had been the moment she'd decided she was definitely not going to be an actor.

"Well, you're going to be great tonight. Just wait until they get a load of you." Genevieve's eyes gleamed in a way that made Cassia's stomach drop.

CHAPTER 6

The interior of the dance studio was only half as full as it had
been for the opening night party. Being a more normal
Tuesday night in town, the main drag was mostly deserted.
Even though the weather was still warm, the early setting of
the sun gave away the coming winter.

About twenty women paced the room under the fluorescent lights, along with a couple of men, including the perky
one with the slicked back hair. This time, instead of a hand-
knit red sweater, he wore a black T-shirt and black jeans.
Cassia caught him staring at the printed cutout of Ricardo and
guessed that had inspired his change of wardrobe.

The studio seemed much dingier without the cheerful
table of food at the back and the feeling of a party from last
time.

Cassia shivered in her jacket in the dance studio and stared
at her reflection in the plate glass windows. It wasn't that cold.
It was probably just nerves. Genevieve had wasted no time
losing her own light jacket and striking up a conversation with
another woman, leaving Cassia to stand awkwardly in the
middle of the room.

She wondered if she could dance the whole night with her coat on.

A few moments later, someone came up behind her and grabbed her upper arms. Whirling, Cassia found Genevieve behind her. "You didn't think I'd let you get away that easy, did you?" Genevieve said with a smile. Cassia hadn't even seen Genevieve leave the woman she'd been talking to.

"Not sure what you're talking about," Cassia said, trying to buy time.

Genevieve held out one hand, palm up. "Coat. Hand it over."

Pursing her lips, Cassia considered refusing, then said, "Oh, what the heck." She took off her jacket, revealing her red dress. Only one other woman was wearing a dress, and hers was a more sensible blue. Cassia felt all the women's eyes turn to her and she held her breath.

After what seemed like an eternity, a teenage girl squealed and came running over. "I love that. Where did you get it? Everything online is so... brown, or blue."

The woman with the blue skirt eyed the girl, who turned red.

"No offense, ma'am," the girl said in a rush.

"I think you just made it worse," Genevieve said in the girl's ear. "Don't call anyone here ma'am."

Despite her irritation, even the woman in the blue skirt laughed at Genevieve's comment, one that turned out to be loud enough for everyone in the studio to hear.

Between the girl's excitement, and Genevieve's joke, Cassia felt her anxiety melt away. Yes, she wasn't used to wearing dresses, but it was turning out to be okay.

Genevieve wandered off with the teenage girl, telling her about online websites for really cool clothes. Cassia decided she didn't need to be a part of that conversation.

The front door of the studio opened again, bringing in the

scent of pine and wood fire from outside. Everyone turned to look with expectant expressions that quickly turned to disappointment. The person entering was not Ricardo, but he did look familiar. Cassia squinted at the man, who looked like he would rather walk back out the door again after the greeting he'd just gotten. Then she realized who he was. Deputy Chester, but out of uniform, instead wearing chinos and a pale blue button-up shirt, surprisingly well-pressed and crisp.

Cassia recognized his discomfort and instantly felt bad. She knew what was like to not feel part of a group. And it wasn't his fault he couldn't compete with the outlandishly handsome Ricardo, even if he was putting in a good run of it tonight.

"Deputy Chester," Cassia said, walking quickly to him and grabbing his arm before he could bolt back out the door. "I didn't see you here on opening night."

Deputy Chester cleared his throat, and his eyes flitted from side to side. "Please, I'm off duty. Just call me Ben."

Cassia's eyebrows rose. "Does Sheriff Andrews know you allow that?" She shouldn't tease him, but she couldn't help herself.

Deputy Chester—Ben—flushed at her ribbing. "Off duty," he said quietly, sidestepping the issue of Sheriff Andrews. He shifted uncomfortably. Several of the women in the room eyed him appreciatively. The only other man there seemed to be already attached to a woman, except for the man with the slicked back hair, who might have been interested in Ricardo himself.

"How about just plain Chester? That way, I won't slip up around Mr. Rules," Cassia said.

Chester looked confused, but then nodded when he realized she meant Sheriff Andrews.

"How did you find out about this?" Cassia asked.

"I, uh, had to work opening night," Deputy Chester said, "but I managed to swing by later and found out about the free week." He gave the first glimmer of a real smile. "I like ball-room dancing."

That surprised Cassia. She couldn't think of anything to say without sounding like a jerk, so just smiled back.

"Welcome, welcome," Ricardo said, clapping his hands. Cassia hadn't even seen him enter. He looked just as amazing as the last time she'd seen him, wearing the same tailored black outfit and man bun. Jane walked with him as he came from the back room, along with another older man also dressed in all black, but with clipped gray hair. He looked like a mirror image of Ricardo, right down to the chiseled jawline, but twenty years older.

"Shall we get started?" Ricardo asked.

One woman in the back giggled. The students crowded toward Ricardo, who deftly backed up and evaded their approach by walking around them to the front of the room.

"But before we get started, let me introduce my wonderful father, Lucas Baros. He is also an excellent dancer and has agreed to help us out here tonight. Some of you might have recognized him from the hardware store," Ricardo said.

"You sure clean up nice," a woman joked.

Lucas nodded graciously. "Hopefully, I will dance just as well," he said, no trace of accent in his voice, and sounding just like any other Midwesterner. Cassia frowned in surprise at that. She had expected him to have an accent like his son, Ricardo.

Ricardo clapped his hands again. "Since we do not yet have enough men, we'll take a line approach at first." Ricardo said, then gave a million-dollar smile. Despite a few grumbling protests, everyone lined up to get the first instructions on a basic salsa.

Cassia and Genevieve took positions next to each other and fumbled to follow the moves. Deputy Chester got pulled further down the line by a cute redhead with curls. He did not look displeased.

"You never told me about your day following the filming," Cassia said to Genevieve, standing next to her as she stared at Ricardo and tried to follow his moves. Seeing him made her curious about Polina. It was hard to imagine anyone being married to that man.

"That's because there was no filming. At least not there," Genevieve said.

"Was the guy who told you about it there?" Cassia asked.

"Yes, and don't you dare say a word. He said he thought for sure they'd be there. Something must have come up," Genevieve said.

"Someone likes you," Cassia quietly sang.

Genevieve reached over and firmly stepped on Cassia's toe.

"Ouch!" Cassia said, giving up all effort to follow the dance and grabbing her foot.

"Whoops. My bad," Genevieve said as she followed the next turn in the dance without missing a beat.

Cassia gingerly put her foot down. Nothing seemed broken. It just hurt a lot. She was definitely going to have to learn to tease Genevieve from further away.

Just as Cassia was getting back into the dance and finally had all the steps together, the door to the street opened again with a slam. The bells swung so hard they fell off and landed with a sad choked ring at the bottom of the door.

Everyone in the room turned as one to look at the doorway.

Polina stood framed in it, the brilliance of her platinum blonde hair highlighted against the black night behind her. She smiled triumphantly.

"Déjà vu," Genevieve said under her breath.

"No kidding," Cassia said, drawing close to Genevieve. There was something about Polina that felt dangerous and unhinged, like a wildcat that had escaped its cage. "I'm not sure I want this much excitement in my life." She glanced at Jane, who was once again working the sound system. The girl's eyes were round, with whites showing around her pupils. Cassia was not the only one Polina terrified.

Polina held up one hand, palm up, waiting expectantly. A moment later, a man stepped out from the darkness behind her and placed a stack of yellow printed flyers in her palm. She curled her fingers around them and then stepped into the room, followed by the man. He looked like a poor man's version of Ricardo: handsome, but not as handsome as Ricardo, tall, but not as tall as Ricardo, even his black shirt and pants were not quite as black as Ricardo's.

But other than that, they looked eerily similar. It was creepy, even.

Ricardo's reaction was not what Cassia expected. Instead of getting quietly calm, or even understandably upset, he seemed amused. The corners of his mouth curled up into just a hint of a smile.

"We have a wonderful opportunity for you all," Polina said, making an effort to sound warm and inviting. She even gave everyone in the studio a smile. The effect was what Cassia imagined would happen if a crocodile smiled at her. It chilled thoroughly, rather than giving assurance.

Polina walked around the room, handing out one flyer to each student in the room. She stopped in front of Ricardo's father and gave him an extra large smile. "Lucas," she said as she slipped him one of the flyers.

He nodded slightly as he accepted it. "Polina," he said, his voice cold.

Continuing around the room, Polina continued with the flyers until she came to an older woman who reminded Cassia of a grandmother on TV, or someone she'd wished had been her grandmother since Cassia had never been lucky enough to have someone like that in her life. Instead of sliding a flyer to the woman, Polina looked her up and down, then shook her head and walked on. "Too fat," Polina said, not even bothering to say it to the woman's face.

The studio was absolutely quiet after that. Polina seemed oblivious to the upset she had just caused. Cassia couldn't stop staring as the elderly woman's eyes glistened with tears. Cassia wanted to yell at Polina, but she felt stuck in place, along with everyone else. Only the women closest to the grandmotherly looking woman stepped closer to her. One hand rubbed her back.

Ricardo took a step forward and stopped himself, his jaw flexing. He breathed in deeply several times before finally speaking. "We do not need any opportunities. Please leave."

Polina turned slowly on her heel to face him. "At least hear me out. I will be filming at the county fair and everyone here, well nearly everyone here," she glanced at the elderly woman she had dissed, "has a role in it. Hollywood has come to you, my dears. Don't lose this chance." It didn't sound so much like an offer as an order. No one else seemed much pleased with it, either.

This time Ricardo approached Polina, blocking her from continuing to walk the room. He motioned her to the door.

The man trailing Polina placed himself between Ricardo and Polina and placed a hand on Ricardo's chest. Cassia sucked in her breath.

Ricardo slowly looked down at the hand and then back up. The man's arm shook a little, but he did not remove his hand.

"Soren, that will not be necessary," Polina said smoothly as she pulled out a folded piece of paper from her front pocket and handed it to Ricardo over Soren's arm.

Ricardo shifted his eyes from Soren to the paper as he took it. He unfolded it slowly and read, his jaw continuing to flex, and then he gasped and retreated a step.

"Just for you," Polina said. "Our little secret. I'll see you at the filming, along with all your… ducklings here." She turned and walked to the door, stopping to allow Soren to open it for her before she stalked off into the night, followed by Soren, who had turned to give Ricardo one last smirk.

"See you at filming," Soren said before the door shut behind him.

The group gave a collective exhale.

Lucas came around and patted Ricardo on the back. "That's over now. You can relax."

Ricardo only shook his head and spoke like a man sentenced to death. "No. We'll do the filming."

Everyone stared at him, their mouths hanging open.

CHAPTER 7

Cassia and Genevieve lay on the blanket laid out on the floor of the telescope dome room that was attached to the back of the mansion kitchen. They laid out a picnic around them of pimento loaf sandwiches, cold fried chicken, and whatever chips were handy, along with bottles of Genevieve's favorite root beer. Above them, the dome was open to the night sky, with a white swath of stars showing what Cassia had never realized before this past month was actually visible to the naked eye—the Milky Way. Growing up she'd thought one could only see it in photographs.

That's the sort of thinking that happens when you're too poor to go to a real telescope observatory. Or the mountains. Or anyplace away from LA or any other large city.

The wind rustled outside, sending the trees flailing and their thin bare branches waving in front of the stars. There weren't many trees, but years of neglect of the mansion had allowed the forest to encroach on the house and interfere with the view from the telescope. Cassia was sure that when the telescope had been constructed, it had looked much different. One wouldn't bother to build such a fancy installation, only to have trees block the view.

The air smelled of the pine trees outside, and also brought in with it the crisp edge of the winter chill coming. Cassia pulled her jacket closer. Soon it would be hot cocoa season.

"What do you think it was all about?" Genevieve asked for about the fourth time. Cassia didn't even bother responding, just rocking her head back and forth on the blanket while staring up at the stars. "I think she's blackmailing him."

"That seems sort of obvious," Cassia said. "Pretty bold to do in front of everybody."

"She thinks we're just a bunch of hicks," Genevieve said.

Cassia shifted on the blanket, putting both hands behind her head. She could see the constellation Orion's Belt, and one of the dippers. She could never remember which dipper was the big one and which the small, which was pretty embarrassing for someone who liked astronomy. But she actually preferred imagining what it was like on different planets and stars out there in the universe rather than looking up at the pinpricks of light high up in the night sky.

"Cassia?" Genevieve asked.

Cassia rolled her head over to look at Genevieve. "Yes?"

"Did you hear anything I said?"

"Yes, we're hicks," Cassia said.

"No, after that. Are you planning on going to the shoot?"

"I guess so. Didn't Ricardo want us to come?"

Genevieve sat up and pulled the six-pack carrier of root beer closer and opened another bottle. "That's what he said. I guess we should do it."

"And I'm guessing you didn't ask him about being a mentor, did you?" Cassia asked.

"Of course not. Another bad night for it," Genevieve said.

"Whatever you do, don't ask him about picking a wife…"

Genevieve just snorted.

57

Everywhere Cassia looked, red dust blew. Chalky red rock stretched out in every direction, reaching out to meet an orange sky in the dusty distance. Next to her, a machine the size of a small car beeped and whistled. It stood on six large barrel wheels, each mounted on its own arm like some sort of strange insect. The machine had two heads, one of which swung around to face her, the shutter inside the camera eye blinking like a wink. It swung the head around again as if pointing to what looked like a square hut on the far horizon.

A hut. On Mars.

Somehow, the hut scared Cassia more than the thought of being on Mars.

Who was in there?

The machine wanted to know that answer too. After pointing out the structure in the distance, it rolled forward, going faster than Cassia thought wise as it bounced on the scattered red rocks on the ground.

"Stop," Cassia said, not thinking about how she could speak on Mars. She reached out, and her gloved hand caught her attention. She was wearing a spacesuit, right down to the fat sausage finger gloves. Reaching up, she felt the glass of her helmet, then a tug at her waist. Horrified, she realized she was connected by a long tube that looked like a vacuum cleaner tube from the stomach of her space suit to the machine that was now rolling away from her.

The machine pulled forward, putting a strain on the tube connecting them. Cassia stumbled forward, not wanting to know what would happen if the tube pulled out from her suit. As if encouraged, the machine sped up, rolling even faster toward the horizon. Cassia stumbled and started to run. Her feet slipped and slid on the rocks and dust lazily lifted from the ground, taking its time to settle back down in the weird way that happens when there's less gravity.

Not that she knew firsthand, but Cassia had seen movies.

For a few moments it seemed she would be okay. She was able to keep pace with the machine—the rover Perseverance she now realized—even though it felt like she was running in a swimming pool, but then disaster struck. She tripped over an especially large rock and went flying forward to land facedown on the ground. Her helmet crazed into a thousand fine white lines. Air started escaping from some of the deeper cracks with a sickening hiss. A moment later, the tube attached to the stomach of her spacesuit gave way to the tugging of the rover and ripped out with a sickening tear, with a rush of air escaping her suit following.

The rover continued rolling off into the distance like a bad dog, the air tube bouncing along behind it like a leash ripped from its master's hand.

Cassia tried to scream, but there was no air for her lungs. The only sound was the rover beeping crazily as it rolled away, the sound getting louder and louder, and not quieter as she expected, confusing Cassia even further.

Soon there was just the sound of the beeping. *Beep, beep, beep*.

Groggily, Cassia opened her eyes. She was in her bed in the mansion, on Earth. The beeping was coming from her phone where it lay on the bed next to her.

Just another stupid dream.

Why couldn't she have great dreams of flying, or living in an exotic alien culture on a fancy shell-world planet? No, what she got were dreams of everything going wrong in the weirdest ways. Even a plain old forgot-to-wear-her-pants nightmare would be a nice change instead of her career challenging nighttime adventures.

She flung an arm over eyes and rolled over.

She hadn't moved from her bed when, several hours later, her phone rang. She roused herself enough to pick it up and stared at the screen. Nate Perauski's office.

Wasn't he at jury duty?

Confused, Cassia pressed the green talk button.

"Hello?"

"Miss Lemon," a formal voice said on the other end.

"Oh, Mrs. Anderson. How are you?" Cassia rubbed her hand over her face, trying to wake herself up.

"Up," said the voice with a disapproving sniff. Cassia stopped massaging her face and held her breath for a minute. She wasn't going to respond to that comment. Luckily for her, Mrs. Anderson wasn't waiting for one.

"Mr. Perauski wanted me to call if we got certain information in this week."

Cassia waited for more but the other end was silent. "Okay," Cassia prompted.

"The information came," Mrs. Anderson said.

Another silence.

"Can you tell it to me over the phone?" Cassia asked. She really missed Nate at that moment.

Mrs. Anderson considered her response on the other end. Mrs. Anderson was not exactly known for being flexible, so it was a real mystery what might happen next.

Finally, after an aggrieved sigh, came the answer. "It is some account information from a bank. You'll have to come in to get the rest. And sign off for it."

"That's not a problem, Mrs. Anderson. I'll be right down. See you soon." Cassia hung up before Mrs. Anderson could say anything further.

Cassia leapt out of bed and went to the curtains and flung them open. The streaming sunshine matched the joy in her

60

heart.

———————

Sweat coated Cassia's neck and back by the time she reached downtown Forgotten Valley, cruising down the hill into town on her bike and feeling like a million bucks. She'd pedaled as fast as she could, feeling motivated for the first time in weeks. It was a good thing she hadn't bothered to shower before leaving the mansion. She'd make up for it with a long bath that night.

The cool afternoon fall air felt great as it whistled down the back of her sweatshirt and pulled at the ankles showing beneath her sweatpants. Despite almost all the leaves having already fallen, the town still looked cute with its old-fashioned Main Street complete with a hardware store and five-and-dime. It was something right out of a cheesy small-town romance movie. It would probably look like a straight-up cliché by the time Christmas came. She'd bet they put colored lights on all the little spindly trees in front of the stores and had old-fashioned caroling, along with ginger cookies and hot cocoa.

And she was sort of looking forward to it.

Not that she would've ever admitted that to any of her cool big-city LA friends if they had asked her. And not that she had many of those sorts of friends, being so busy with school and work and all.

School! She grinned from ear to ear as she pedaled on the street, thinking of what schooling she could hit after this year in town. If she got enough money, she wouldn't have to worry about where she could get a scholarship, not now when she had the golden ticket. Some thought schooling was a way to earn more money, but Cassia knew better. School was a way to get to play with all the toys no amount of money could buy, at least no amount of money any normal person could get a hold of. No regular person, or even a mildly wealthy person, could ever afford to build fifty-four gigantic telescopes high in the Andes Mountains in Chile, but an astronomy student at a prestigious university could get in to use them.

And prestigious institutes like tuition money.

The schemer in Cassia knew that just getting into a school was a much lower bar than having to get in and get them to give you scholarship money.

She could at least do the first.

She would do it.

Pressing down hard on the pedals for extra emphasis, Cassia raced down the hill into town, taking a winding route through the back streets to avoid all the stop signs getting to Nate's office.

Finally, she pulled to a stop in front of Forgotten Valley Lawyers, LTD. Nate's office light was off, but a dim light from the main lobby showed through the front window under the huge gold letters. Mrs. Anderson was still there.

Triumphant, Cassia looked around for a place to lock her bike.

There were only meters along each side of the street, and a stop sign half a block away.

Cassia considered using a meter for exactly thirty seconds before deciding Mr. Rules himself, Sheriff Andrews, would probably stroll around the corner at the exact second she secured her bike lock to it.

Someday she was going to have a car and really use those meters for a use he approved of.

She shook her head. Was she really fantasizing about paying a meter?

Nevermind that.

Taking a deep breath, Cassia grabbed the front door with one hand and rolled her bike in with the other. She gave an apologetic smile at Mrs. Anderson's surprised expression.

"Sorry, sorry… but if I locked it up out there, Sheriff Andrews will pop a gasket."

Mrs. Anderson pursed her lips, but finally gave a minute nod and pointed to the corner furthest from her. Cassia rolled the bike there and set it against the wall, behind the row of always empty, or so it seemed, chairs in the lobby.

Mrs. Anderson looked timeless as always. She must have been close to seventy or eighty, but it was hard to tell for sure. Her violet-blue suit looked new, but that style was in again with the bouclé material and matching skirt and jacket, and for all Cassia knew, Mrs. Anderson could be wearing an original from the first time that look made the go-around in the 1950s. Her light blonde hair was wound up tight in a beehive that would have made the B-52s jealous.

Actually, her style was growing on Cassia. What was it with this town and women who just did not care what others thought? Between Genevieve and Mrs. Anderson, Cassia was going to have to rethink her own biases about small towns and who lived there.

"I'm glad you made it," Mrs. Anderson said, then glanced at her watch, the implication being that she had somewhere else to be.

"I pedaled as fast as I could. You know I'll be faster once I get one of those cars," Cassia said with a huge smile that only earned a weak smile in response.

"I suppose," Mrs. Anderson said. She lifted a large blue and white USPS Express mail envelope that had already been opened. "It was addressed to the firm, and I've the authority to open all business mail."

Cassia nodded. She hadn't thought to challenge that.

"Take it," Mrs. Anderson prompted when Cassia only stared at the envelope. "It won't bite you."

After a nod, Cassia strode forward and took the envelope.

Peering inside, she saw a small blue book the size of a passport and a sheaf of papers.

"Mr. Perauski was able to overnight the will and your notarized identity papers we keep on file. You'll just need to visit a branch prior to taking out your first withdrawal."

Mrs. Anderson's words faded to the back of Cassia's perception as she reached into the envelope and pulled out an old-fashioned bank book. In blue slanted ink, the last entry had more significant digits than Cassia had ever seen on anything that wasn't a physics problem.

CHAPTER 8

What had been a refreshingly breezy afternoon took on a distinct chill as the sun lowered to the horizon. Cassia shook her hair out of her face as she pushed her bike into the wind toward the diner. It was now suddenly unpleasant being outside, and it seemed the rest of the citizens of Forgotten Valley had taken the hint and were nowhere to be seen. Most of the shops were closed and dark, and those that were still open had only dim lights doing little to fight the oncoming night. Cassia was the only person on the street. It only made the dim street feel more ominous.

Even Mrs. Anderson had zoomed out of town in the biggest baby blue Chevy coupe from the seventies that Cassia had ever seen, giving Cassia a honk and a wave, and nearly a heart attack from the gigantic beast of a car going by.

Finally reaching the diner, Cassia lifted her bike up to the sidewalk, and then toward the front door. She'd forgotten to talk to Trent about a place to park her bike. He shouldn't mind if she brought it just in the entryway for a moment until they figured it out.

She hoped.

But instead of finding the normal warmth and chaos and fantastical smells of delicious food when she pulled open the door, she found the slight antiseptic smell of the floor cleaner and the sight of all the tables with their chairs on top, just as it would look at closing time. Not a single customer in sight. Not even any staff. Cassia checked her phone, feeling she'd entered a time warp. No, it wasn't ten o'clock; it was only 6 pm. What was going on? Why had Genevieve told her to hurry for her shift if there was no one even here?

"Hello?" Cassia called.

No response.

She tried again, louder.

A banging from the back answered her second call, and a moment later Genevieve came out through the swinging doors to the kitchen. "You're here. Excellent. We're just about ready," Genevieve said, untying the black half apron she normally wore at work to hold her waitress pad and pens.

"Ready for what? What's going on?" Cassia asked. "I thought I was—"

"Work's canceled tonight. We've got more exciting things going on," Genevieve said as she shoved her apron under the counter and pulled out the huge black duffel she used as a personal bag. "Time to change. It's a good thing I keep extra clothes at work."

That didn't sound good.

Cassia shook her head, but Genevieve ignored her as she set the bag onto the counter and dug into it.

"I have a better idea of your size now. This should be perfect." Genevieve held out a bundle of clothing to Cassia.

Cassia didn't move.

Genevieve cocked her head. "What are you waiting for? Come on. Come and get them." She waved the clothes at Cassia as if they were a delicious treat she was offering to a ravenous puppy.

66

"Yeah, um, maybe I should talk to my boss about my shift tonight…" Cassia said, trying to buy some time.

"No worries. The diner's closed tonight. He's coming with."

Now Cassia was really confused.

"Coming with where? What is going on, Genevieve? Your message said to just hurry. I thought it was so busy that even you needed help."

That elicited a genuine laugh from Genevieve. "Not to be mean, but I don't think I would be texting you for that."

"It did seem strange," Cassia said, agreeing with her.

"We're going down to the Wild Horses Banquet Hall. Apparently they had a last minute cancellation and the movie guys were all over that. Plus, Polina promised Trent to throw the wrap party at the diner if he and Jack, the other diner cook, could bring some other guy friends to the shooting of a rehearsal scene. Apparently it's hard to get guys as extras for a dance movie."

Cassia remembered how few men were at the dance lessons. "I bet."

Genevieve gave Cassia a wicked look. "And Ricardo and Lucas are going to be there too. More family fireworks."

"Lovely," Cassia said. She wondered if bribing Trent to stay open for the night instead of going to the rehearsal shoot would be worth the money.

Genevieve's blue Honda sped down the black two-lane country road, its old headlights barely lighting up the road winding deep through the pine trees. Genevieve contentedly hummed under her breath, her face aglow in the yellow light from the dashboard. Once again, Cassia shifted uncomfortably in the passenger seat, wearing something of Genevieve's that was both scratchy and short. At least it only itched where it covered her.

At least this outfit came with a matching scarf. Too bad she couldn't use it as a skirt; it might have been larger than the one she was wearing. Genevieve had tied the scarf on Cassia's head and told her it was all the rage.

They'd shoved Cassia's bike into the backseat so she could get a ride directly home after the night's events, but that just made Cassia even more uncomfortable as it forced her seat so far forward that her knees nearly touched the dash.

Cassia consoled herself by thinking about the bank book and how much she looked forward to getting home later to examine the contents of the envelope she'd gotten from Mrs. Anderson. She'd not had much time at the law office before Genevieve's frantic text had come. Cassia had only had time to say goodbye to Mrs. Anderson, shove the envelope into her backpack, and get her bike out of the office with Mrs. Anderson on her heels with the key to lock up.

Everyone had someplace to go, it seemed.

But first, Cassia had to get through what promised to be a very strange night.

"I don't understand," Cassia said. "I thought you like Ricardo. Why are you happy he's being forced to do stuff for this Polina woman?"

Genevieve glanced over at Cassia. "I'm not *happy* he's being forced to do anything. I'm just not going to miss a chance to witness any of it. I mean, a famous influencer, and a Hollywood movie all here in Minnesota? Wild horses couldn't keep me away."

"Does that have anything to do with the name of the place?" Cassia asked.

Genevieve looked at her blankly.

In the distance ahead, a pair of headlights approached

them on the two-lane highway. Genevieve did not seem to notice, instead focusing on Cassia and her question.

Cassia sat up as much as she could and pointed forward. "The road. The road!" Her voice actually squeaked. She'd thought they'd made up squeaking voices in books, but as Genevieve shifted her eyes forward and swerved them away from the pair of oncoming headlights just in time, it occurred to Cassia that squeaky voices were a very real thing when scared.

A fact she could have done without learning.

Cassia breathed heavily and gave thanks she hadn't lost her bladder control over that one.

"What are you talking about?" Genevieve said, seemingly completely unfazed by their close call.

"The name of the hall—Wild Horses. Nevermind. It was a stupid dad joke," Cassia said, reminding herself to not talk so much to Genevieve when she was driving. Or at all, if she wanted them to arrive alive wherever they were going.

"Oh. Well, it's a great hall. Tons of people are going to be there, I'm sure. Just you wait and see."

Great. More people to look ridiculous in front of. If Cassia had had more room, she would have slumped all the way down to the floor.

———

The Wild Horses Banquet Hall was an enormous tin warehouse of a building, low and sprawling, that took up half a field of what looked like corn stubble in the background. An enormous sign in the front blinked two life-sized neon horses, one red and one blue, flashing in some pattern Cassia could not discern, to the forest of pine trees around them.

The sign looked like it belonged in downtown Las Vegas, not in the middle of the woods in northern Minnesota.

A narrow road of blacktop ended in a broad gravel pad that was the parking lot. Parking also spilled to the field behind the structure. It looked like a hundred cars could stay here.

The whole setup was completely incongruous with the setting. It would've looked even more lonely except there were half a dozen pickup trucks and vans taking up much of the parking lot. Some of the pickup trucks sported generators in their back beds that were hooked by long snaking black cables to industrial-sized lights on high stands that Cassia could see spilling out around the back of the building. It must be part of the movie shoot. For some reason, they were working out back, outside, at night.

"This is a crazy huge building in the middle of nowhere," Cassia said to Genevieve as the Honda rolled into the parking lot. Genevieve picked a spot far away from the building and the noisy generator trucks.

"Cheap property taxes," Genevieve said as she killed the engine. "It's outside the township lines."

"How do you know—"

"It pays to be friends with Roger. I tell you, that man knows everything," Genevieve said as she flipped down the visor and checked her lipstick. Satisfied, she flipped the mirror up again. "Isn't this exciting? Everyone's going to be here. This is just crazy."

Cassia had to agree with that, at least about the crazy. "Are they expecting us to be outside, because I'm not dressed for that."

Opening the car door confirmed Cassia's thoughts. It was freaking cold out there. That was a problem with clear nights. They're beautiful, but they let all the heat escape up into the night sky.

"Don't worry about it. We'll be fine. You know I have clothes in the car."

Cassia bit her lip to not make a comment about the clothes she'd seen—and worn—from Genevieve's car.

They crossed the loose gravel of the parking lot to the building. It looked dark inside, so they walked around the side of the building. Voices murmured and grew louder as they rounded the corner.

Cassia had seen a few movie shoots here and there in Los Angeles. They sometimes shot on the street. It was always lots of people and trucks, and you rarely actually saw any of the actual filming, so she wasn't surprised to see so many people standing around, most of them looking as cold and uncomfortable as she felt. What did surprise her was that *everyone* was standing around. It didn't look like anything was happening at all.

"Hi," Genevieve called out to the nearest group of people. "We're here for the shoot as extras. I think we're a bit early, like maybe an hour."

"We are?" Cassia hissed at Genevieve. Being on time was one thing, but showing up an hour early to stand around in the cold was another entirely.

Genevieve waved her hand behind her at Cassia to hush her up. Cassia bit her lip and decided she would get her revenge another time. Something really, really good.

An older man with leather gloves hanging out of his back pocket approached them. "Actors aren't expected yet. Maybe just wait over there," he said, pointing to the section of the wall further away from the main group of people standing around with some expensive looking equipment. "The wrangler should be around for you soon."

Great, like they were cattle.

Cassia just nodded, not wanting to argue with the man. Maybe if they stood over there long enough, she could convince Genevieve they should go home. This didn't seem nearly as glamorous to her as it did to Genevieve.

Genevieve nodded as well, but as soon as the man turned, she pushed Cassia toward the spot he had indicated, but then walked off to another group of people standing around. Cassia heard her greeting and then their voices dropped. Hurrying to the spot along the wall, Cassia pulled her cloak close and tried not to shiver.

Moments later, Genevieve joined her. "Apparently the director and the AD, whoever that is—"

"Assistant director," Cassia said, helpfully.

Genevieve tilted her head at the unexpectedly supplied information but continued on. "They can't find Polina. Apparently she's the head producer person, whatever. They don't want to go on without her organizing the setup. Wouldn't that be the director's job?" Genevieve asked, suddenly realizing Cassia might know more about movie shoots than she thought.

"They direct the actors, but they don't really supervise the crew that much," Cassia said, waving to the massive groups of people around them. The question of where they even put up that many people popped into Cassia's head as she looked around at the group. This was not a small shoot. She was impressed despite herself.

"Wow. The drama continues," Genevieve said, looking around and nodding.

Or doesn't, Cassia thought, looking at the entire crew standing around talking.

"I'm going to see if I can get more information," Genevieve said. She walked out before Cassia could stop her. Cassia thought about joining her to talk to the strangers, then decided to stick where she was. She didn't have the social skills to smooth over someone else getting mad at her for being in the wrong place, at least not like Genevieve did.

Bored of standing in one place, Cassia started pacing along the wall, walking in long ovals along the concrete wall and trampling down the weeds that grew there. The gardeners were not very conscientious along the side of the building, or whoever was doing the mowing.

In each circuit, Cassia walked further, getting closer to the far end of the building. It was relatively dark there, far from the high bright lights mounted by the movie crew just around the corner from the front. The tall weeds threw long shadows, hiding what was further away, which was gradually getting revealed as Cassia trampled them down with each pass of her pacing.

Reaching the far corner of the wall of the long low building for the first time, Cassia glanced around the back and was startled to see the flash of something silvery in the dark, shadowy weeds behind the building.

Someone yelled behind Cassia. Startled, she turned around and saw Ricardo and Lucas come around from the front of the building to the side. They walked through the middle of the bright movie lights. Around them, crew members who recognized Ricardo were coming over and laughing and joking and reaching out to shake his hand. They weren't going to make him stand in the corner relegated to nobody extras.

Cassia turned around to resume her pacing, but her foot got stuck on a root and instead of turning neatly, she ended up sprawling backwards and landed on something hard that hurt her back. Swearing, Cassia reached down, but instead of finding a rock, she found a high heel with its pointy toe jammed in her back.

Then her fingers touched something cold.

There was a foot and an ankle inside the offending shoe. Cassia pulled her hand away quickly and looked back as she scrambled away.

Polina lay sprawled in the weeds, her blonde hair and silver jewelry shining in the low light.

Cassia screamed.

CHAPTER 9

Weeds damp with condensation slid sickeningly along Cassia's bare ankles and calves as she backed up, stumbling through the undergrowth, trying to get away from the horrible sight of Polina sprawled in the grasses. The woman almost could have been sleeping, except for the unnatural angle of her neck, barely visible in the darkness behind the Wild Horses Banquet Hall.

Cassia stopped screaming and tried to catch her breath as she felt her heart racing inside her chest, each beat thumping in her ears. She shivered.

Crew members ran over, led by Genevieve. Ricardo followed the group, striding on his long legs and accompanied by Lucas. Cassia thought for a moment she should stop him, but before she could organize her thoughts, it was too late.

"What? What?" Genevieve asked.

Cassia pointed, then turned away.

Genevieve stared at the body, while a crew member peered over her shoulder then swore at the sight before turning to wretch into the bushes.

The crew crowded around, whispering furiously.

74

Ricardo pushed in, took one look at Polina, and rushed in to kneel by her side and check her for a pulse.

Lucas watched the whole scene, a strange expression on his face. He did not join his son by Polina's side.

A familiar hat bobbing in the crowd caught Cassia's attention as she tried to focus on anything but the broken body she'd just seen. Before she could get his name out, Sheriff Andrews' booming voice cut through the crowd. "Everyone BACK!"

A stunned silence met the sheriff's demand, followed by the crowd opening up a path. Sheriff Andrews strode through the newly made space, his back ramrod straight and his badge shining brightly in the reflected light from the movie set. His crisp uniform stood out in the sea of casual jackets and hats. Deputy Chester followed sheepishly after, most decidedly not in uniform, instead wearing a rather loud one-piece red velvet bodysuit peeking out from underneath a long parka. At least it looked like red velvet in the low light. It would have been a daring outfit in the disco era in New York City. Cassia could not help but stare as he walked by. Clearly Deputy Chester had come for the movie filming.

Sheriff Andrews strode to the body and kneeled on the side opposite to Ricardo. "I said back," he barked at Ricardo, who held up his hands and shook his head, then rocked back to his feet, having already checked for a pulse and finding none. Sheriff Andrews checked Polina's neck, but quickly pulled back his hand at the coldness of the body. Polina was dead.

Very dead.

He stood again. "No one leaves." He motioned to Deputy Chester. "Make sure everyone stays, and get them in some sort of order. I'll call for assistance." Sheriff Andrews stared at the crowd, as if he could pick out the guilty party just by looking at them, but then stepped away to pull his phone from his belt. On his way out of the circle, he walked by Ricardo and pushed a finger into Ricardo's chest. "Especially you.

Make sure you don't go anywhere. You were touching the body."

Dazed and offended, Ricardo spluttered, "I was checking for a pulse," but Sheriff Andrews had already walked on.

Genevieve pulled Cassia to one side. "What happened?"

"Nothing happened... Not that I saw. I was just walking and tripped over that... her," Cassia said, feeling a little ill. She'd never seen a dead body in her life, even her parents' funeral had been closed casket, but now, within a month, she'd seen two dead bodies. Weren't the cities supposed to be the big scary places? Small towns were supposed to be cute and safe.

Whoever sold that story was a big fat liar.

———————

Cassia sat on a vinyl and metal conference chair, pulled from the stacks of chairs lined along the wall behind her in the broad, empty banquet space of the Wild Horses Banquet Hall. It had not been set up for anything. The huddled tables and chairs around the edges of the room left a vast depressing space in the middle. Apparently, all the filming was going to happen outside, but once Polina's body had been discovered, someone had called the owner of the venue and he'd come and unlocked interior rooms so the craft and movie people could come inside and keep warm. Leaving the place was not an option. Sheriff Andrews wanted everyone to stay until he had a chance to talk to them.

All of them.

Cassia squinted in the bright fluorescent lights. They weren't especially powerful, but after spending forty-five minutes outside in the dark, her eyes were still struggling to adjust to any normal light. A shiver overcame her, and she pulled her jacket closer. Even being inside had not yet banished the chill she felt inside and out.

Around her, scattered in groups in the vast space, were some of the other movie people. Deputy Chester had blocked the extras who showed up later for their call times from entering the property, reducing the traffic in the crime scene area and leaving mostly the professionals who looked like they had flown in from Los Angeles just for this film work. They were easy to pick out from the locals by their brand-new coats and jackets that looked just a little too expensive.

Some were packing up expensive camera gear, but most were sitting around in the same generic chairs as Cassia, whispering among themselves. Everyone was waiting to be called into the kitchen area that was being used as an interrogation room. One particularly stressed looking young man with bleach blond hair and black roots and holding a clipboard had tried to organize everybody, but most had ignored him and he finally gave up and sat alone staring into space. He worried Cassia a little.

"Here," Genevieve said as she pushed a foam cup of coffee into Cassia's hands. Cassia took it gratefully. It was only lukewarm, but she was glad to have it. "Powdered cream," Genevieve said, making a face. "I haven't had that in ages."

"Did you find out anything from Deputy Chester?" Cassia asked as Genevieve pulled a chair close and sat with her own cup of coffee.

"Yeah, they called into the Twin Cities for help on this one, but bigwigs probably won't get here till morning. They have to deal with everything local until then," Genevieve said. That meant the body and dealing with all the witnesses. Even the normally unflappable Sheriff Andrews had had a sheen of sweat on his brow when he had walked by earlier just after they opened up the interior of the building.

A few moments later, sirens sounded outside. Cassia was curious if that was an ambulance or more cop cars, but not curious enough to get up from her chair. She'd find out soon enough, she thought cynically.

"How's Deputy Chester holding up?" Cassia asked. He had looked very uncomfortable trying to direct people and show some authority while out of uniform. Sheriff Andrews had snorted at the sight of Deputy Chester in his velvet red dance outfit, but had only gone outside and got a spare Mountie hat from his trunk which he had shoved on Deputy Chester's head before going back into the kitchen with his pad of paper and voice recorder for interrogations.

The double glass doors to the outside swung open and two unfamiliar deputies walked in, both young and bristling with energy. They only hesitated a second to take in the crowd before walking back to the kitchen area without a word to anyone. They must have talked to Sheriff Andrews by phone and known exactly where they were going.

"Looks like help is here," Cassia said. "Maybe we'll get home by dawn."

Genevieve laughed. "Why do I somehow doubt that?"

Cassia frowned. That was not a good sign. Genevieve would know better than she. There were probably some rules Sheriff Andrews wanted everyone to follow and that took a lot of time.

A lot, a lot of time.

At Cassia's unhappy look, Genevieve pulled her chair even closer. "Who do you think did it?"

That was the big question, wasn't it?

Cassia tried to subtly scope out the group around them. There had to be somewhere between thirty and forty film people here. Who knew what their relationship to Polina had been? Probably not good. The few times Cassia had seen Polina, she'd managed to anger every person in the room, and even made a woman cry with just a few choice words.

And her stepdaughter Jane had looked downright scared.

"I have no idea," Cassia said. "Seems like it could be nearly anyone."

"Got that right. I thought we were going to see blood when she was pulling that stuff with her stepdaughter the other day. That little girl did not like her," Genevieve said, then threw back the rest of her coffee and then stared at the bottom of the cup balefully like it had personally betrayed her by no longer being full.

"I'll be right back," Cassia said. She got up from her chair and put her empty cup in the seat where she'd been. There had to be bathrooms around here somewhere.

She went to the long hallway that led in one direction to the kitchen and in the other direction to a series of small rooms that must be offices. A few doors down, she found what she was looking for, the ladies' room.

Pushing open the heavy industrial door, the bathroom lighting was even worse than the banquet hall. The banquet hall chandeliers had at least attempted to create some atmosphere that wasn't completely lost, even with the brightness turned all the way up, but the bathroom was a different story. Straight-up blinding bright fluorescent lights glared at Cassia from eye level around the mirrors. She squinted and waited a minute for her eyesight to adjust. The hint of a migraine pulsed in the back of her left eye. Great.

Glancing in the mirror, she saw how she looked with the scarf Genevieve had insisted she wear. She looked like a big yellow banana.

"Great," she muttered under her breath as she pulled off the scarf and shoved it into her coat pocket.

While she waited for her eyes to settle, she heard heavy banging. It sounded like it was coming from a room next to where she was. She thought that would have been the men's room, but hadn't really been paying that much attention.

Muffled yelling came with the banging. Cassia realized

someone was hitting the wall for emphasis with the yelling, which was causing most of the noise.

Someone was very, very unhappy.

Tiptoeing across the room, she found a spot between the mirrors where she could put her ear against the wall. It helped, a little, but not enough to pick out actual words. The walls must be surprisingly thick for such a place. She would've thought they'd been made as cheaply as possible.

She tiptoed back to the entry door and slowly opened it, holding her breath as if that would keep it from squeaking on its hinges. Luckily, it was new enough, or well-maintained enough, that the door opened silently. She stuck her head out and checked the hall.

No one was coming.

The sound was louder in the hallway. It was coming from the men's room next door.

Cassia glanced down the hallway to the main banquet room once again to make sure no one was coming before she stepped out into the hall and stood near the men's bathroom. She pulled out her phone to make it look like she was checking something on it in case someone came by, but she was really just staring at the blank screen and listening as hard as she could.

A slam happened inside the men's room, which sounded like a hand slapping up against the metal hand dryer. "I told you, no good would come of this," a voice said with a thick accent.

Ricardo's voice.

Who is he talking to? Whoever it was talked more softly, their response only a low rumble.

"No, I didn't get it. What do you want me to say? I wasn't there," Ricardo said, his voice even louder.

More of the low rumble talking followed. She couldn't catch a word of the second person's speech.

What were they talking about? Could this have something to do with Polina, or something else?

"No! I will not. You will not ask such a thing again," Ricardo said, the rage in his voice making Cassia shift uncomfortably from foot to foot outside the door. She did not want to be standing here when he came out. There was no one else around and she felt suddenly very vulnerable.

Another banging came from inside the men's room, and Cassia lost her nerve. Turning quickly, she started walking back to the banquet area. Too soon, the men's room door flew open behind her and Ricardo stormed out, walking past her swiftly to the banquet area. He didn't even give her a glance as he passed her in the long hallway.

Cassia exhaled slowly in relief. She let her pace slow, only to jump as a low voice said nearly in her ear, "I think you dropped this."

She turned to find Lucas holding out the yellow scarf that must have fallen from her pocket. Reaching out for it, she looked up to his eyes, which narrowed at her.

Cassia gulped.

CHAPTER 10

Standing in the empty hallway of the Wild Horses Banquet Hall, Lucas gave Cassia a smile that did not reach his eyes. She noticed he had a lot fewer wrinkles than she expected of someone who had an adult son and a near teenaged granddaughter. The sound of distant chattering from the main room behind her reached Cassia, making her wish more than anything she was back there with a crowd of other people, and not alone in this hall with a man who suddenly seemed much younger and angrier than she had thought before.

He stepped forward. Like his son, Ricardo, Lucas was also well-built. His muscles bulged beneath the trim black shirt he wore. This was a man who worked out, not someone who spent all day in front of the TV eating nachos.

Above them, one of the fluorescent lights flickered in and out, one of its parts needing replacing, and only adding to Cassia's sense of unease. She did not like being alone in this hallway with Lucas, but desperately did not want to give him any reason to suspect her of spying on him.

Which is exactly what she had been doing.

Looking down, she grabbed the scarf and busied herself

shoving the resistantly fluffy polyester length into her jacket pocket, trying to do a better job this time so it wouldn't fall out again. She hoped Lucas would move on while she was doing that. Instead, he stood there and waited, watching her as if he had something else to say. Taking a deep breath, she looked up again and spoke in a rush. "Thank you so much. I would have been really sad to have lost that."

She turned to leave, but before she could take a step, Lucas grabbed her arm and stopped her.

"Are you okay?" he asked.

Flustered, Cassia gave a small laugh. "Of course I am. Why wouldn't I be?"

He tilted his head. "Oh, I don't know. Someone died tonight."

"Oh that," Cassia said, immediately regretting it. "Yes. Upsetting. Definitely upsetting. See? I can't even talk right now, I'm so upset."

"Was there anything else upsetting you?" Lucas asked her. His eyes bore into hers. They were an unsettling dark gray color, not the brown she had first thought. Very cold looking. She took a step backwards, despite herself.

Act normal. Act normal. Act normal, she told herself, trying to make herself stop retreating and giggling like an idiot.

She might as well tell water to not be wet.

"No," Cassia said, her voice actually breaking, "nothing else is bothering me. I should go." She hooked a thumb back to the banquet hall area, hoping to remind him that there were a lot of other people in this building, as well as reassure herself. "My friend is waiting for me. And the sheriff, too, I guess."

"I see," Lucas said. "Well, if you ever need anything, you can always talk to me."

Cassia was definitely not a good enough actor to keep the surprise off her face at the offer from someone she'd only met once. "You're too kind," she said, and then turned and walked quickly back to the main banquet room. Her back itched as she imagined Lucas staring after her.

––––––––––

Cassia was further surprised to see a lot fewer people in the main banquet hall. At least one group was completely gone. Their conference chairs were left in an empty circle, not even put away when they'd gone. Genevieve sat at their pair of chairs, sipping another cup of coffee and holding a full one for Cassia. Outside, blue and red emergency lights flashed through the double glass doors. More emergency vehicles had shown up.

Cassia walked to Genevieve and accepted the cup of coffee Genevieve held out to her, then sat down next to her. Even under the fluorescent lights, Genevieve still looked put together. Was there any situation that took this woman by surprise? Cassia was beginning to think not.

"Where is everyone?" Cassia asked. She took a sip of coffee while waiting for Genevieve's response. This one tasted better. Her eyebrows shot up.

"Better, right?" Genevieve said, lifting her coffee to indicate what she was talking about. "They don't lock the banquet hall's fridges. They have real cream, unlike these movie folks from LA. I thought California was all about health food and all that? All those people have is junk food and candy."

"Your latest blockbuster, brought to you by sugar," Cassia said, not surprised. "No one is going to work for twelve hours on a movie set for an apple or bean salad, but give them a dozen donuts and you might have some inspiration." She'd heard enough about how those things worked from classmates who did extra work for cash and entertainment.

Looking around while drinking her coffee, Cassia spied

another group of now empty chairs further in the back. There were definitely a lot less people there.

"Seriously, where is everyone?" Cassia asked.

"More deputies came from the next county over. At least four of them are taking statements," Genevieve said.

"Whoa. And Sheriff Andrews is okay with that?" Cassia asked. She had only known the man for about a month, but even she knew that was wildly chaotic for him. She expected him to want to supervise each questioning.

"I'm sure not, but this isn't his jurisdiction, apparently. It's the next county over, and the guy in charge just looked like he wants to get home and get to bed. He's not too thrilled about having to be here till morning when the Twin Cities folk get here."

"I don't blame them. I don't want to be here till morning either," Cassia said.

"If you had been here earlier, we could've gone. Or maybe not. You were the person to find the body. Either way, Sheriff Andrews was asking where you were. I told him the bathroom," Genevieve said.

"Bingo," Cassia said, holding up a thumb. She briefly considered telling Genevieve about what happened with Ricardo and Lucas, but there were too many people around. Besides, it was probably nothing. She was probably imagining how weird it felt. Besides, Lucas had a point; someone did die that night. Everything was bound to feel weird and scary.

"There you are," Sheriff Andrews said, his deep voice rumbling over Cassia as he stood in front of her. She jumped and gave a small squeak as she spilled coffee on her lap, still hot enough to sting.

It was a night of squeaks. Lovely.

She looked up to Sheriff Andrews standing in front of her with his hands on his hips. He looked about as pleased with her as Lucas had a few moments earlier. What was with the crabby men in this town? Or towns, since apparently they were in a different one here, a whole different county in fact.

"You know, we never have murders up here, but you've been around what, a month? And found two bodies. Don't you think that's a little suspicious?" Sheriff Andrews said.

Cassia's face flushed a deep red, the heat rising through her hairline and making her scalp tingle. Suddenly she felt very, very short in her chair and wanted to stand up but couldn't. Sheriff Andrews was standing so close and she would have had to push him back to get room enough to rise. Instead, she was forced to crane her neck to look up at him, something that quickly became extremely uncomfortable.

"I just found them. It's not my fault," Cassia said, hearing the stupidity of what sounded like a child's excuse for something as serious as finding a murdered person, or apparently murdered people.

Maybe Polina wasn't murdered. Maybe she just fell in the wet grass and slipped and broke her neck.

Cassia shook her head. It would have to had been a serious fall to make Polina's neck look the way it had when Cassia had seen her. It didn't even seem possible from standing.

"Is this the one who found the body?" a smooth voice asked. A young man in a very well fitting deputy uniform came and stood next to Sheriff Andrews, beaming at Cassia despite the somberness of the occasion. If Sheriff Andrews was good-looking, this man was a marvel. He was a slightly younger, more svelte, and thicker-haired version of Sheriff Andrews. Cassia couldn't help but gape at him. Especially at his cut cheekbones. She expected the good-looking folks to be with the movie people from California, and not the local deputies, but once again, she was wrong.

Sheriff Andrews scowled.

Cassia quickly schooled her expression to neutral. Unhelpfully, Genevieve giggled next to her and gave Cassia a not-so-subtle elbow to the ribs. "Ouch," Cassia said to Genevieve and shifted away from the woman.

"It is," Sheriff Andrew said to the newcomer. "I was about to take her back to make a statement."

The newcomer waved off Sheriff Andrews as if swatting away a fly. "No need. I'll take it from here, Deputy."

Sheriff Andrews narrowed his eyes at the young man. "It's *Sheriff* Andrews. I'm the senior officer on-site."

The young man slowly pivoted on his heels to give Sheriff Andrews his full attention, while not dropping the small smile he still had on his face. "Nice to finally meet you face-to-face, Sheriff Andrews. My name is Deputy Waters. We've spoken on the phone several times. While I agree, you are a *senior* officer," the way he said senior not exactly flattering, "the fact is you are from a neighboring principality. You don't have jurisdiction in Bellard County. We do. I will be taking this young lady back to make a statement."

The two men faced each other, neither one budging. Cassia could almost see the black clouds above each of their heads as they faced their opponent. All that was missing was a red cape and a matador... but which one was the bull?

It was getting late. It felt like midnight, though Cassia knew it couldn't be that late, and even Cassia's temper was starting to fray, but this was ridiculous.

"Why don't I give a statement to both of you at the same time," she said, finally. Not that she really wanted to spend more time with the two of them at each other's throats, but it seemed the quickest way to get things over with. "I really want to go home and get some sleep."

Deputy Waters cleared his throat at Cassia's proposal. Suddenly, neither he nor Sheriff Andrews would look at her.

"What?" Cassia asked. "What's going on?"

"I don't think you understand the situation," Sheriff Andrews finally said to Cassia, sharing a look with the other deputy that Cassia could not interpret except it made her anxiety spike.

"What situation?" Cassia asked shakily.

"Sheriff," Deputy Waters said, a warning tone in his voice.

Ignoring Deputy Waters, Sheriff Andrews went on. "It seems someone thinks you might have had something to do with Ms. Jan-Baros' death," Sheriff Andrew said.

"Me?" Cassia said, yet again squeaking. At the same time, Genevieve said, "Who?"

Sheriff Andrews gave Genevieve a withering look, then motioned to the back of the building, as if they could all see through it. "Ms. Jan-Baros is the woman who died tonight."

Genevieve took that in, her mouth a small "o" of surprise. Finally, she sprang to life, fully indignant. "Cassia, kill Polina? No way! She didn't even know the woman. Besides, we were together the whole time."

Deputy Waters gave Genevieve a smile at that and tipped his hat. "Yes, well, we're gonna need your statement, too. Don't you go anywhere."

Cassia and Genevieve exchanged panicked looks.

CHAPTER 11

Deputy Waters and Sheriff Andrews led Cassia back to the kitchen area. Two other deputies came and got Genevieve at the same time, leading her off in a different direction, apparently to question her at the same time. There'd be no comparing stories, not that there were stories to compare, since Cassia didn't plan on lying about anything.

Industrial-sized lights dotted the ceiling of the kitchen area, sending a blaze of fluorescent light shining down on the stainless steel tables and shelves. It looked spotless and sterile and cold. Cassia shivered.

They had set up an interview area in a back corner of the enormous room, at what looked like a stainless steel prep table that had been pulled from the corner and several stools pushed up to it. Sheriff Andrews motioned for Cassia to take a seat at the far stool and then placed a handheld recorder on the table in front of her and pushed the record button.

Somehow, this felt worse than when he had questioned her at the mansion. Maybe that was because then she had been sitting in one of the parlor rooms of her own house, or soon to be house, mansion, whatever. Here—this place—felt like it could be the prison she might have to go to someday.

No, never.

She had not done anything wrong.

Deputy Waters pulled up a stool and positioned himself close next to Cassia, almost in line with the recorder on the table. Sheriff Andrews frowned at that and pulled up his own stool on the other side of the table, his further distance a decided disadvantage. Cassia found the whole thing aggravating because she could not look at both of them at the same time, instead having to constantly shift her gaze between the two of them. Why couldn't they just sit next to each other like normal people?

This was going to be impossible.

"Okay, Miss Lemon, is it?" Deputy Waters asked, reading from a clipboard in front of him. "Like the fruit, really?"

Cassia's brows knit. He was not looking so cute anymore. "Cassia Lemon," she said as coldly as she dared, resisting the urge to say anything about his last name of Waters. Bottled waters. Running waters. Suddenly she was in grade school and the childish insults ran amok in her head, but she resisted the urge to say anything. But honestly, who as an adult would make fun of someone else's last name?

Deputy Waters inhaled to ask a question, but before he could, Sheriff Andrews barreled in by reading Cassia her rights. Deputy Waters scowled, but didn't stop the sheriff. Sheriff Andrews took full advantage of that by continuing straight on to his first question. "So you say you got here about fifteen minutes before you found the body? Do you know what time that was?"

Sheriff Andrews waited for an answer. His stare made Cassia nervous..

"It was after dark, but not too long after the sun had set. Maybe 8 pm?" Cassia said.

"You don't know for sure?" Sheriff Andrews asked. "Did you check your car's clock when you arrived?"

"Um, no," Cassia said. "Genevieve's radio light is burnt out... in her car," she said to clarify at their confused looks. "And I didn't bother checking my phone when we arrived. I wasn't really paying much attention since she was sort of in charge of getting us here on time. This was her thing, believe me, I was just going along with it—"

Sheriff Andrews raised a hand as if he was gonna stop Cassia from speaking, but Deputy Waters leaned in smoothly and said, "Let her go on. We've got the time."

Cassia shut her mouth with a snap. She wasn't stupid. She knew he said that because he wanted her to ramble on and say something, anything, they could use against her.

But that shouldn't be a problem, since she hadn't done anything, right?

Her breath hitched in her throat. The sterns looks of the two dead-serious law enforcement officers shook her confidence that the truth would protect her. Suddenly her stool felt too high and rickety.

"What did you do when you got here?" Sheriff Andrews asked. He wanted her to walk nearly step-by-step through their short walk around to the side of the building where the movie crew had set up. His frown at her lack of details unnerved her.

"It was dark. We went back there. They pointed us to go stand by the wall out of the way. That's all I remember," Cassia finally burst out, frustrated.

"Then how did you end up alone behind the building while your friend was elsewhere?" Deputy Waters asked, earning glares from both Cassia and Sheriff Andrews. Unfazed, Deputy Waters raised his eyebrows, waiting for his answer.

"Because I got bored and wandered back there while pacing. Genevieve had gone to talk to someone at the time."

"So when you found the body, you were actually alone, and had been for some time."

Cassia stared at him, her mouth open. Finally she said, "Yes, I was alone."

――――――

After more questions, and what seemed like an hour later, a young deputy came in and whispered in Deputy Waters' ear. He, in turn, stood and motioned for Sheriff Andrews to follow. All three of them left the kitchen, leaving Cassia to squirm on the hard stainless steel stool and stare around at the cold and empty kitchen.

It was probably a lot more pleasant during the day when filled with people and activity. Now it felt like a morgue.

A few moments later, Sheriff Andrews and Deputy Waters came back. "You're free to go. For now," Sheriff Andrews said. "We'll have a statement for you to sign later today or tomorrow. And remember, I know where you live."

Cassia grimaced at that. He didn't need to remind her.

Sheriff Andrews ran his hand over his face and readjusted his hat, and then waved her out of the room. She was not the only one the night was wearing on. Only Deputy Waters seemed as energetic as he had been when they started talking. As handsome as he was, something about him rubbed Cassia the wrong way.

Feeling oddly off-balance at the sudden change in their attitudes, Cassia hesitated leaving the kitchen, but turning back to check, neither Sheriff Andrews nor Deputy Waters gave her a glance. They were deeply engrossed in a quiet conversation between themselves.

She squared her shoulders and left the kitchen. After only a few wrong turns, Cassia found the main room of the banquet hall, and stumbled in to find that nearly everyone was gone except for a few antisocial stragglers, each sitting by themselves in the corners of the room, slumped in their uncomfortable chairs and staring at their phones.

Cassia's and Genevieve's chairs were still where they'd left them near the middle, complete with the empty coffee cups on top. Cassia walked to her chair but didn't even have a moment to sit down before Genevieve followed her into the room with an enormous dramatic sigh.

"Well, I'm ready to go home. What about you?" she asked Cassia. The people remaining looked up from their phones and glared at Genevieve. They were not free to go yet. Genevieve saw their looks and held up her hands. "Sorry. Sure they'll call you soon. It was so much fun. Definitely worth it."

"Shhh" Cassia hissed at Genevieve. No sense antagonizing people.

"Sorry. Those guys were getting on my last nerve," Genevieve said to Cassia. "Did you notice they've got probably seven deputies and sheriffs and whatever in this group, and only one woman? And they've got her standing outside."

Cassia stared. She'd never actually seen Genevieve angry before. For some reason, it had never even occurred to her it was possible, but now that she'd seen it, she was in a hurry for it to be over.

"Yeah. You know what a great place to talk about this would be? Home, with a pimento loaf sandwich with about half a bottle of mustard," Cassia said.

The lines in the middle of Genevieve's brow eased. "You know, that's the best thing I've heard all evening. Let's go."

———

Cassia and Genevieve made it out of the building as far as the far end of the parking lot where Genevieve had parked, now eerily empty and quiet, before red siren lights showed up in the distance, the light reflecting off pine trees. The oncoming car looked a few miles away, but it was a narrow road and there was no sense trying to drive it, only to have to scramble to find a place to pull over. They might as well wait for it to arrive there first so they could then drive safely away.

Outside, all the former activity of the movie shoot was long gone—the massive lights were down, the generators shut off, and most of the people and vehicles gone. It was quiet enough to hear crickets. Only a half dozen dark county sheriff cars stood parked at odd angles, as if parking spots didn't exist for them, and the yellow crime scene tape that stretched along the far side and back of the building, stretched between a few more sheriff vehicles. A single woman patrolled back there. She had nodded at Genevieve and Cassia when they'd exited the building, but otherwise hadn't said a word.

How had Genevieve known she was out here? Cassia wondered. They had both been inside that whole time. She'd thought so anyhow. Cassia added that question to the list she had going in her head about exactly what had happened that night. If Genevieve knew anything, she was going to find out.

The vehicle drew closer, finally driving to the lone splashes of white light from the few large overhead fixtures the Wild Horses Banquet Hall had sprung for so their customers wouldn't be completely in the dark in the parking lot. Cassia recognized Deputy Chester, even with his hat on, as he drove past them to pull up to the double glass doors of the front entrance. His funky red velvet outfit shone oddly in the low light. Apparently, he'd not gotten the time to go home and change.

He beeped the sirens for a second, then turned off the car and got out. Opening the back door, he reached a hand in and helped someone out of the car.

Soren. The guy Chester helped out was the same guy who

had been with Polina the last time they'd seen her, looking like a polished little imitation of Ricardo.

But this was a very different Soren—a muddy and disheveled one. One of his shirt tails hung pulled out and loose, and his skin showed through a tear in his trousers.

Genevieve scooted closer to Cassia, squinting at the scene in front of them. They were too far away to see it all that clearly. "Is that Polina's sidekick guy, and does he have hand-cuffs on?" Genevieve asked Cassia in a whisper. The night was so still, however, that both men turned to look at Cassia and Genevieve at the sound.

"Oh crap," Genevieve muttered, then gave a huge smile and wave, and then called out more loudly, "Have a good night."

Luckily, at that moment, Sheriff Andrews and Deputy Waters came out of the Wild Horses as if they'd been waiting for the two men to arrive. The four men stood and talked quietly for a few moments before Deputy Waters pointed out Cassia and Genevieve standing and watching. The men turned to look at them, then went into the building as a group, leaving Cassia and Genevieve alone except for the lone deputy on the far side of the building guarding the crime scene.

"Well, that was strange," Genevieve said.

Cassia had to agree.

CHAPTER 12

Cassia relaxed as Genevieve's car wound through the trees and then emerged to finish the approach to the Mandress mansion. Home, at least for now. Even the dark tower reaching to the clouds was a welcome sight.

If it was a dark and shadowy place when the sun wasn't shining, it was even worse when night fell. The sky had clouded during the drive home, and the mansion and the surrounding grounds lurked in the murky darkness.. Why hadn't the Mandresses put up more lights? Money could not have been the issue, even if it was an issue for Cassia right now.

But Cassia could change that. She decided the first thing she needed to make this place homier would be lots of exterior lights. Lots of them. She didn't want any dark corners where people could lurk or secretly crawl about. That was another thing that she could spend her money on when she got her hands on some.

Genevieve pulled around the front curve, then parked her car on the pavement just past the door.

"You promised me food," Genevieve said as she unhooked her seatbelt and got out of the car.

Stepping out of the car, Cassia felt surprisingly achy and sore all over. Maybe she had been tenser than she thought when she was sitting there getting questioned by the deputy and the sheriff.

"No worries," Cassia said, not bothering to explain about her dwindling food supplies. Genevieve was her ride to the grocery store anyway, so she might as well see when the next trip was due.

They got Cassia's bike out of the backseat and made it to the front door.

Fumbling in her bag, Cassia pulled out the key but then stopped when she heard a noise coming from inside the mansion. A bang, followed by some scratching.

Scratching?

Ah. Cassia relaxed, knowing what that might be.

Genevieve held on to Cassia's bike while Cassia struggled with the lock and finally got the door open. Just as she thought, Miss Mansfield stood in the entryway staring up at her, her back arched and her eyelids slightly lowered. That was not the appearance of a happy cat.

Flipping on the light, Cassia glanced at the lower half of the inside of the front door. Deep lines etched the paint job, showing impressive force from Miss Mansfield in marking the door. Cassia didn't think they had been there earlier.

Miss Mansfield sat down and stared at Cassia, blinking her golden eyes and looking quite pleased with herself.

"I'm sorry I was late with dinner," Cassia said, "but that was uncalled for."

Genevieve nudged Cassia forward into the entryway so she could bring the bike inside and shut the front door. The house was at least twenty degrees warmer than outside, so it felt good to get inside.

"Something wrong?" Genevieve asked, staring back and forth between Cassia and Miss Mansfield.

"No, nothing's wrong," Cassia said. At the same time, Miss Mansfield rose again and delicately stepped over to Cassia and then put one paw on Cassia's toes while looking straight up at Cassia.

"Hey," Cassia said.

Miss Mansfield responded by putting a second paw on the same foot, now the weight of the front half of the cat's body firmly on Cassia's big toe.

"Hey!" Cassia said.

Genevieve giggled, watching the interaction.

"I said I was sorry," Cassia said.

Miss Mansfield leaned slightly forward and tried to get her rear paw on the same foot, and then her fourth paw. It was an impressive balancing act, even for the small cat that was only seven or eight pounds.

And seven or eight pounds is a lot of weight when it is focused into a small area by tiny feet pressing directly on one's foot.

"Ouch! Off, off, off," Cassia said, shooing and waving her hands at Miss Mansfield. For some reason, she was not quite brave enough to actually push the cat off her foot, even if she felt ridiculous for being slightly scared of the tiny animal.

As if bored with the interaction, Miss Mansfield hopped off Cassia's foot and then walked primly toward the kitchen, her tail straight up with a tiny hook at the end. She walked slow enough that the hint was clear; they were to follow her and fix Cassia's error as soon as possible. Dinner was very late.

Genevieve shrugged. "We're going there anyway." She leaned Cassia's bike against the hallway wall, being careful to not scratch the delicate pastel blue paint.

Cassia and Genevieve followed Miss Mansfield into the kitchen, and Cassia went directly for the pantry stuffed full of cat food and grabbed a can, pulling the lid open, then going to get a dish to lay it out on. It was only after she set down the dish of wet food at Miss Mansfield's special eating place—which took the whole of what was supposed to be a desk area in the kitchen—did Cassia hear the slightest of purrs coming from Miss Mansfield, even though the cat still refused to look at her directly.

Meanwhile, Genevieve had made quick work of pulling all the most delicious things out of the fridge and spreading them on the center island. She knew exactly where all the dishes and utensils were, and had a sandwich made and in her mouth before Cassia could even sit down to rest her feet.

"What about me?" Cassia asked.

Genevieve just motioned to the spread of food in front of them. "I didn't know what you wanted," she said around a bite of food.

"Hrmp," Cassia said. A month ago, Genevieve would have made her sandwich. There was such a thing as being too comfortable with each other. Cassia grumbled, but made her own sandwich of sunbutter and gobs of jelly. She wanted something sweet and comforting.

When Genevieve had finished half of her sandwich, she went to the fridge and pulled out two bottles of root beer, popped the caps, and gave one to Cassia.

"I don't get it," Genevieve said. "Why were they so sure we were somehow involved, and then just let us go?"

They had talked about this on the way home, and nothing about it had made sense. But even after getting some food in them, and being able to think straighter, it still didn't make any sense.

"Did the guys interviewing you say anything about why Deputy Waters and Sheriff Andrews said that to us?" Cassia asked.

"No," Genevieve said. "They just kept asking me what I was wearing. It was really annoying. Especially since they could see what I was wearing."

"They didn't ask me about that at all," Cassia said, frowning. Why the difference?

"Ugh. I'm just sick of it all. And I still haven't asked Ricardo about social media and all that stuff." Genevieve picked up her sandwich again and took an enormous bite, taking out her frustration on her chewing.

"Yeah, the good days of asking that question might not exist anymore, or at least for a while," Cassia said as she surveyed the food on the counter, trying to figure if anything appealed for seconds.

"You're telling me," Genevieve said. "Do you think this is going to affect the dance studio?"

"Why would it? Polina had nothing to do with it."

"You would think," Genevieve said, agreeing with Cassia. "But she was always there, it seemed. Or maybe we were just that lucky. Anyway, Ricardo and Lucas and Jane might be affected by it."

"Lucas didn't seem to care, even if Ricardo did," Cassia said. Just saying Lucas's name made her feel uneasy. The first time she'd seen him in the dance studio he had just looked like a nice older gentleman, but after her encounter in the hallway at the Wild Horses Banquet Hall, she wasn't so sure. She hadn't had that icky feeling from someone in a long time. That anxious feeling of not feeling safe.

Cassia gave an involuntary shiver.

They ate in silence for a few minutes.

"I just can't believe someone died. Again," Genevieve said.

"Stop," Cassia said. "Now you're starting to sound like Sheriff Andrews. Are you going to blame me for this one too?"

"Of course not. Girl, I think you're tired," Genevieve said.

Cassia nodded. There was truth to that.

Genevieve brought her plate over to the sink and rinsed it off, spying the picture Cassia had stashed on the counter earlier in the week. After drying her hands, Genevieve picked it up and stared at it. "Oh cool, Tricky Dick."

Cassia spluttered, nearly spitting out her sandwich. Holding a hand over her mouth, she managed to swallow. "What?"

"Tricky Dick," Genevieve said, holding up the picture to show Cassia and pointing at it with her other hand. "Why do you have a picture of him?"

"Who?" Cassia asked, more confused than ever.

"Richard Nixon. The former president of the United States?" Genevieve asked, laughing a bit at Cassia.

"Oh," Cassia said. Embarrassment mixed with surprise. She thought Genevieve was her same age. Why did she seem to know so much more history?

As if Genevieve could read her mind, Genevieve said, "My mom was obsessed with him. I don't know why, but we had lots of books with his face on the cover. And doing this." Genevieve put the photo down and then held up her two hands with the index and middle finger up in bunny ears.

"Like they do in Korea?" Cassia asked, confused.

"Yep," Genevieve said. "Though I don't think they got it from him. Peace sign and all that, probably."

Genevieve turned back and picked the picture up again and stared at it. "Holy cow, he's with Senior Mandress in this photo." She stared at the photo even closer. "Was that taken here? Wow, wow, wow, the president of the United States was in this house. That's wild. Where did you find this photo?"

"In a book in the library," Cassia said.

"Ooooh, more mysterious messages from the books. Was it in one of those really old volumes? One of the antique ones probably worth a lot of money?" Genevieve asked.

"No," Cassia said, just now realizing the strangeness of it. "It was in a newer book. Someone must have put it there rather recently."

The next morning dawned bright and sunny, the birds chirping loudly enough to be heard through the thick fabric over Cassia's windows, waking her. Rising from the bed in a rush to throw open the curtains, she disturbed Miss Mansfield, who was sleeping curled in a ball at her feet, and earned an irritated meow.

"Sorry," Cassia said.

When the sunbeam hit Miss Mansfield, the cat instantly stretched her long legs out in front of her to meet her rear paws, also stretching forward, her irritation instantly forgotten as the warmth of the sun heated her dark fur.

Everything seemed better in the sunshine. Cassia felt more powerful, and more in control of her own destiny.

Besides, she learned last month the danger of relying on someone else to do all the investigating, especially if her own future was on the line.

If someone was going to say she had something to do with some crazy murder—if it was a murder—well, that was just not cool. She was gonna have to do something about that. No way she was taking the blame for something she did not do.

Grabbing her phone off the nightstand, Cassia typed up a quick text to Genevieve and sent it off. They both worked the evening shift at the diner that night. They had all day to take care of other things, and Cassia had a list ready to go.

A few hours later, she and Genevieve were driving down Highway 71 to the big box store with all the goodies. The traffic was light midmorning, and between the streaming sunshine and the crisp fall air, it felt like a perfect day. Yesterday's event seemed like a distant nightmare. Cassia rolled down her window and put her hand out to feel the air flowing over it, pretending her hand was an airplane. It had been one of her favorite things to do as a kid, and she did as much as she could when people weren't getting at her to roll the window up because of the air-conditioning.

"I like your plan," Genevieve said. "Plus, it's always good to see Roger. We get cookies and he gets more fish. Win-win for everybody."

"Excellent," Cassia said, as she rolled her head lazily on the headrest to stare at Genevieve. "I've got another surprise too. Do you mind if we stop at a bank while we're in town? I've never been there before, but I looked the directions up."

"A bank?" Genevieve asked, surprised. "Does this mean what I think it means?"

"Maybe," Cassia said, patting her backpack that held the bankbook she'd gotten from Mrs. Anderson. She finally decided to show Genevieve. She had to trust somebody, and she needed a ride to the bank anyhow. Of all the people Cassia knew, Genevieve would probably be the least jealous of anybody. Plus, Cassia was looking forward to the first time she could like pay for someone else's grocery bill, even if the groceries were being bought to help her investigation.

"Whoo-hoo!" Genevieve said. "You're buying lunch."

"You know it," Cassia answered.

The Honda sped up and raced down the freeway.

CHAPTER 13

The thick green pile carpeting in the bank lobby absorbed all the sound, leaving it a quiet place where people only whispered, much like a library. The deep green of the carpet matched the tone of the dark walnut wood counters and desks of the tiny branch office. Miniature chandeliers hung in intervals over the small space, matching perfectly the decadence of the decor.

Two men in dark navy suits sat behind the teller counter, reminding Cassia of the male secretaries from A Christmas Carol. Other employees worked at low desks along the back wall. The only other customer was a white-haired little lady sitting across one of those desks, being helped by a female employee also wearing a dark blue suit, but this one with a skirt.

The whole setup looked like it would have fit in a hundred years ago.

"Whoa, what is this place?" Genevieve asked, drawing the attention of everyone inside.

A woman in the apparently required blue suit rose from behind one of the low desks along the back wall and came to greet Genevieve and Cassia as they stood in the lobby gawping. "May I help you?"

It was the most polite and yet unpolite sentence Cassia had ever heard, but she squared her shoulders and soldiered on. There's money in them there hills, the saying went, or something like that. She belonged here, even if no one who worked there thought so.

"I believe I have a bank account here," Cassia said. The woman did not immediately react, waiting for Cassia to say more, and Cassia could feel the two men at the teller counter staring at her too. She rushed on. "I inherited it. My lawyer's been in contact with you and sent you the required documentation but, apparently, I had to come down here for something. To sign something." Cassia shut her mouth and forced herself not to say another word. She was babbling. It was embarrassing.

Cassia glanced down at her faded jeans and wished she'd thought to wear something else. Anything else that didn't have holes in the knees. To be fair, any bank she'd been in before had decidedly not looked like this one.

"Do you have an account number, or any documentation with you, perhaps?" the woman asked.

Cassia dug in her backpack and pulled out the envelope from Mrs. Anderson. The woman took it gingerly and opened the flap, pulling out the sheaf of papers and reading all the legal stuff Cassia didn't quite understand. She knew there was an account number on there, so hopefully that was what this woman needed.

Apparently it was, because the woman nodded and then motioned for them to come sit in front of her desk along the back wall while she pulled the keyboard close and started typing on it.

"Will you be making deposits to this account?" the woman asked.

Blushing, Cassia said, "Not just yet."

The woman continued typing. The name plate on the desk said Monica Flourique.

"I'm printing the document for you to sign now. We'll just need an ID to make sure it matches the one we now have on file," the woman said as she continued to type.

"No problem," Cassia said. She unzipped her backpack and reached inside for her wallet. "I'd like to take out some cash today too, please."

"How much?" the woman asked.

Cassia bit her lip while she thought. She had a lot of things she had to pay for, but running around with a pile of cash was not the smartest thing either, considering she had to bike nearly everywhere. "Can I get a cash card, and then maybe a thousand dollars now?" Cassia said, thinking she had shown great restraint.

The woman stopped typing and looked at Cassia with her eyebrows up. "Did your lawyer let you know how much money was in this account?"

Cassia couldn't help but smile. "Yes. Well, no, his secretary did. She gave me the bankbook."

"The bankbook?" The woman looked confused.

"Yes," Cassia said, a sick feeling growing in her stomach. She pulled out the small book and opened it to the last entry, then passed it to the woman. "This is what I was given."

Genevieve looked inside the book as Cassia passed it over and gasped at the number she saw. Cassia glared at her.

The woman examined the book, flipping a few pages back and forth and checking the account number on the front. She went back to the last entry and stared at it, then ran her finger along the line. "Did you happen to notice the date of this last entry?"

Shaking her head slowly, Cassia's sense of foreboding grew.

"It is from 1971. I'm not surprised. We haven't used bank-books in quite a while…"

The woman's voice faded from Cassia's consciousness as all she could think about was the year 1971, which was more than fifty years ago. Which was also before she'd even been born.

"Excuse me," Cassia said, interrupting the woman. "What is the balance now?"

The woman frowned. She hesitated, then grabbed a pen from an ornate wooden holder and scratched out most of the zeros in the last entry of the bankbook, wrote in some numbers in a heavy scratching hand, and handed the bankbook back to Cassia.

Cassia stared at the tiny number now scribbled into the neat book, ruining both the beauty of the prior entries and her dreams of having enough money.

Cassia slumped over the enormous shopping cart and pushed it slowly through the aisles of the warehouse store, her feet clumping along like a depressed six-year-old. At 11 am on a Thursday, the few people in the store were of the older, retired variety. Cassia and Genevieve pretty much had the vast fluorescent lit warehouse with goods stacked four levels high and spread all over the broad concrete floor all to themselves. It was too early for most of the lunch goods at the food counter, so the store didn't even smell as good as it usually did. Normally, Cassia would have gotten a slice of pizza as part of the shopping trip, but she was too depressed to even want to eat anything.

Genevieve came back from one aisle over and deposited an enormous six-pack of goldfish shaped crackers into the basket of the ridiculously large cart. "They're out of the Swedish fish. This is just terrible."

"How does this guy not have malnutrition?" Cassia asked.

"What?" Genevieve asked.

Cassia pointed to the cart. "Who survives on eating fish, and fish shaped foods; what was the other thing? Oh yeah, candy. Malt balls."

Unperturbed by Cassia's grumpiness, Genevieve just laughed. "He does just fine. Besides, I'm sure it's not all he eats, it's just like what he wants other people to give him. You know, like gifts."

"Right," Cassia said, slumping even farther over the cart until her head was resting on the push bar as she pushed it.

"Stop it," Genevieve said, putting her hands on her hips.

Cassia stopped walking.

"That's not what I meant," Genevieve said.

Cassia groaned.

"Stop being so depressed. The lady said there was an account at some other bank this account used to do transfers to, and she thought that the other account was also in Mildred's name. Nate can probably get it all straightened out when he gets back from jury duty," Genevieve said, trying to cajole Cassia into a better mood.

"The other bank account was probably that thief Sarah's account. The money's probably gone forever," Cassia said.

Genevieve threw up her hands. "You're not normally like this. What happened to your big plans for the day?"

"They were scratched out at the bank."

Genevieve crossed her arms and stared at Cassia.

Cassia lifted her head and turned the other way and rested it back on the bar so she wouldn't have to see Genevieve.

Genevieve huffed and walked away.

A few minutes later, Cassia felt a sharp pinch above her left elbow, followed by a burning twist she recognized from grade school playground pranks. "Ouch!" She stood up and rubbed the skin above her elbow. "That's not funny—" she said as she turned around and stopped when she saw the enormous ice cream cone Genevieve held out to her.

It must have had five scoops on it. Chocolate, vanilla, strawberry, and a few flavors she couldn't recognize except for they looked like caramel and had nuts in them. There was even a maraschino cherry jammed on top of the stack.

"What is that?" Cassia asked in awe.

"It's your emergency ice cream. And you have to eat the whole thing before you're allowed to talk again. Or think. Or have another depressing thought. You're alive, things are fixable, and ice cream is a thing. Be. Happy," Genevieve said. She grabbed Cassia's hand and wrapped Cassia's fingers around the cone.

Cassia stared at the impossibly large stack of ice cream on the cone she now held.

"Take a bite," Genevieve said, command in her voice. "Now."

Cassia did.

Maple nut. The top flavor was maple nut. She closed her eyes and took another bite, feeling something like relaxation spread down her back.

———

"Is it possible to have an ice cream hangover?" Cassia asked as they pulled in front of Roger's yellow house and got out of Genevieve's car. The house's two-story old-fashioned structure and grounds were just as wild as she remembered, with garden gnomes and complex machinery spinning in the breeze filling the yard. Actually, there seemed to be more of it. A huge open area in the front garden had more garden gnomes—some with space suit helmets—standing in a circle around a replica of the Mars rover, but instead of having two cameras mounted on it, the rover had small metal fans spinning in the breeze. It was cool and weird all at the same time.

And totally unexpected. Who would expect a homemade model of a billion-dollar piece of equipment in someone's front yard?

"What is this?" Cassia asked, pointing to the display and feeling excited for the first time since leaving the bank. "Does he like space stuff?"

Genevieve gave her a shrug. "I dunno. You'll have to ask him."

"Hellooooo," the man himself called from the upper window of his house. His white hair looked even longer than last time, and flew even more in all directions, like a human version of a dandelion puff. He waved cheerfully at Genevieve. "Good timing. I've been having a craving for some crunchy fish."

"Got ya covered, my man," Genevieve called back as she slapped at the stuffed bag slung over her shoulder.

Roger pulled back into the house and shut the window. A few moments later the front door swung open, and he bounded out to them barefoot and wearing enormous overalls, with a huge straw hat shoved onto his head. He bubbled with happy energy.

Cassia was fascinated. How did one get to be that joyous and comfortable in one's own skin?

"Hello my new friend," Roger said to Cassia, then gave Genevieve a big hug.

"You're in a good mood today," Genevieve said. It was true. Roger had been much more reserved the first time Cassia had met him.

"I am. I am," Roger said, beaming.

Genevieve put her hand on her hips and waited. Roger just grinned back. Cassia stood awkwardly to one side. There was some information dance going on here that she didn't quite understand, and decided it was just better to let them go through their steps.

"Okay, fine. I'll ask. Why?" Genevieve said, putting on a mock show of being aggrieved.

"I'll tell you over lemon cookies and tea in the back," Roger said.

"Deal," both Cassia and Genevieve said at once. Both Genevieve and Roger turned to Cassia, surprised.

"What?" Cassia said defensively. "I remember those cookies. They're good."

The lemon cookies were more than good. They were delicious. Like little lemony tarts with a thin layer of crunchy nut crust on the bottom. It had been a day of delicious things to eat, and that alone was making it much better than yesterday.

Roger, Genevieve, and Cassia sat in Roger's backyard, perched on the comically oversized garden furniture nestled in the bushes and wind chimes. Of the summer flowers, only the marigolds were still hanging on, their lush orange flowers stubbornly refusing to give in to fall just yet.

Cassia and Genevieve's purchases from the big box store surrounded Roger like some really strange alter devoted to the god of fish shaped food. And malt balls. Cassia decided to ignore how weird that was. It was totally worth it if Roger could help them.

"So what's the good news?" Genevieve asked once they were all settled.

"The Massive Museum O'Science commissioned me for a full-sized replica of the rover for a summer exhibit to celebrate the new moon missions. I'm going to make it more functional than what I've got out front, since they're paying me to do it." Excitement gleamed in Roger's eyes. "They're going to have it move a bit. Something about interactive stuff with kids."

"Oh, wow, that's fantastic. How did that happen?" Genevieve asked.

"Someone from the place saw my work in their friend's yard."

"That's really cool," Cassia agreed.

"So enough of my good news. Why are you over here with so many gifts?" Roger asked. "Not that I mind, but you know, I know something's up."

"What, me?" Genevieve asked with her hand over her heart.

Roger just looked at her. Cassia coughed on her cookie at his look. He was not dumb, that was for sure.

"Yeah, someone died last night," Genevieve said.

"Oh no, sorry to hear it," Roger said, looking confused.

"It didn't look like a natural death," Cassia said, by way of explanation. "We were hoping you could help us get—"

"Maybe do some 'repair work' for the sheriff's office. You know," Genevieve said with air quotes, cutting Cassia off and giving her a "be quiet" look.

Biting her lip, Cassia frowned and slid to the back of her enormous chair, her feet now dangling in the air. Again, she was missing something here. The oversized chair was starting to feel appropriate for her kid-like mistakes.

Roger looked sadly between the two of them. "I'm afraid you might want these crackers back. The sheriff's office has cut off my contract work with them. Something about uniform county standards for contractors that the northern counties are doing."

"What?" Genevieve said, shocked.

Oh boy, Cassia thought, this doesn't sound good.

CHAPTER 14

"Girl, you've got no game." Genevieve said as they pulled up behind Smith's Diner and Deli, just ten minutes before their shifts. It had been a long day already and Cassia was not looking forward to a night on her feet, forgetting people's orders—not on purpose, of course—and then apologizing to everyone in town. The Smiths had been especially rude about it. They were probably still mad they didn't get to have their after-party for touring the Mandress mansion after she inherited the place. Or would officially soon.

The back parking lot was full. Genevieve had to park on the spot that also shared the dumpster. Trent let her do it at night when the truck was sure not to come.

Just walking through the parking lot was a bit of a challenge due to the enormous size of the pickup trucks jammed in back there. Cassia had to admit these people had some driving skills. It took that and then some to manage to park a huge truck in a spot designed for a little car. Whoever painted the lines must have been more used to city cars than country vehicles.

As they got closer to the building, the smell of steak meatballs wafted out to Cassia. In only a few short weeks, Thursdays had come to be her favorite day to eat at the diner, even if working that busy day wasn't such a hot experience.

"What are you talking about?" Cassia asked as she lugged her bag with her waitress uniform and shoes in it. She was going to have to hurry to change in time.

"You don't just say things bluntly, like 'Go spy on someone...' " Genevieve said like it was the most obvious thing in the world. "It's called plausible deniability. It's on all the procedurals on TV."

Cassia narrowed her eyes at Genevieve. "Are you sure you didn't kill Polina? You seem to know all the tricks."

"I know you're joking," Genevieve said as she opened the door for Cassia.

Disturbingly, Cassia realized she had no idea where Genevieve had been right before Cassia had found the body. Of course Cassia was joking.

Wasn't she?

———

Cassia was wiping down the last of the tables in the dining room when she heard the bells to the front door of the diner jingle. She'd been counting down the seconds until she could lock the front door and be officially closed, but whoever had just come had beat her by less than a minute.

"We're about to close," Cassia called, without looking up. It had been dark outside for an hour already, so she hadn't seen them walk by on the sidewalk and approach the place. She was quickly learning to hate this part about later fall. No one should have to go home in the dark.

A deep voice said, "I'm not here for food."

Cassia looked up. Sheriff Andrew stood just inside the diner, his arms crossed. Gray puffy bags hung under his eyes, and his clothing was wrinkled. Uncharacteristically so. If his clothes weren't outright pressed, they were usually pulled so tightly across his muscles that wrinkles didn't have a chance, but it looked today like time had won out over his normally pristine look.

Standing slowly, Cassia fiddled nervously with the cleaning rag in her hands. "Then what are you here for?" she asked.

"You were supposed to come down to the station today and sign your statement," he said.

"Oh. I thought you would call me or something when you wanted me to be there," she said.

"Genevieve as well. You know where she is?" Sheriff Andrews said, as if Cassia had not spoken at all.

Cassia hooked a thumb to the back. Genevieve was helping to shut down the kitchen, as Jack had to leave early again, something Cassia wanted to know how he managed to do so often, frankly.

"Do you want us to come there now?" Cassia asked.

Sheriff Andrews uncrossed his arms and sighed, then ran his hand over his forehead, pushing his hat back. "No. Tomorrow is fine. Just make sure you show up sometime during the morning. Got that?"

"No problem," Cassia said. "I'll know from now on that I'm supposed to come in and sign a statement right away. The next day."

Sheriff Andrews eyed her. "Is that a joke?"

"No…"

"Because I sincerely hope you don't plan to be involved in any other crimes in Forbidden Valley."

"I wasn't involved in it," Cassia said, her voice cracking. "Besides, it wasn't in—"

He glared at her for a brief second before turning and exiting back out the door, leaving her to face the swinging bells alone.

"—Forbidden Valley."

She threw the rag down on the wet table.

———

"Well that was fun," Cassia said sarcastically as she walked out of the sheriff station to where Genevieve was leaning against her car and staring at her phone. It was a beautiful sunny Friday morning in Forbidden Valley and the town was relatively busy with cars filling the street and using nearly every meter. People walked the old and cracked sidewalks, many of them ones Cassia had never seen before. Some of them must be from the cities down south, up here starting an early weekend get-away in the scenic north.

It was nice to actually see what the town looked like so early in the day, even if Cassia was dead tired from staying up too late the previous night. She'd been looking for more notes in the books in the library of the Mandress mansion. Of course she hadn't found anything else, but it had been a good stress relief for her insomnia.

"Hmmm?" Genevieve said without looking up.

Cassia waited for Genevieve to look up from her phone, but she didn't. Instead, she started typing something on it.

"At least we didn't have to go to Bellard County for that," Genevieve said without looking up.

"Yes, considerate of them to work together," Cassia said with a bit more sarcasm than she intended.

Bored, Cassia looked around. There were no street benches on this block, hidden back from the main drag. It had been built more recently than the hundred-year-old buildings that lined Main Street, so instead of cute benches with intricate iron backs, this street had a lone garbage can and various street signs. It was rather depressing, but Cassia somehow doubted

Sheriff Andrews bothered noticing what the boulevard looked like outside his station.

"So you're done," Genevieve said, finally looking up and glancing at Cassia.

"I am. How did you get out here so quickly?" Cassia asked.

"Speed-reading classes. Those transcriptions had lots of errors. Did you notice that?" Genevieve asked.

"Yeah. Is that how witness statements are supposed to work? They just transcribe our interviews?"

Genevieve shrugged. "It's in our own words, I guess." She gave Cassia a sly smile. "Guess who got us in the Saturday classes?"

Cassia cocked her head at Genevieve. She didn't mean... oh yes she did, Cassia realized, judging by Genevieve's smirk.

"Dance classes," Cassia said, not quite believing it.

"What else?"

"Don't we go on Tuesdays?"

Genevieve pushed off from the car. "And now Saturdays. There is no way I'm waiting till Tuesday to see what is going on over there. Besides, I haven't given up on asking Ricardo about social media. How do you think I found out about the additional classes on Saturday?"

"We have to pay for these?"

"Don't you get depressed about that," Genevieve said. "These are my treat. I'm thinking of it as my entertainment for October. And a business investment."

"What business?" Cassia asked, confused.

"I haven't thought of it yet, but it's going to be something. Internet something. Can't be a waitress for the rest of my life. Maybe I could be a media consultant."

Cassia couldn't see Genevieve sitting still in front of the computer that long, but she didn't say anything. Maybe Genevieve would find a way to do it on her phone, on the go. Somehow, she could see that happening.

Dreading the answer, Cassia asked, "What time do we have to be there?"

Genevieve laughed. "Not that early. Just make sure you go to bed after we get home from work tonight."

Cassia groaned.

———

Genevieve was a full-on big fat liar and Cassia was never gonna believe another word she ever said again.

Ever.

Cassia looked out the peephole of the front door of the Mandress mansion with Genevieve on the other side, grinning and holding up two coffees and a white pastry bag. Actually, she was opening the pastry bag and trying to tilt it up to the peephole so Cassia could see all the powdery goodness inside.

A horrible big fat liar bearing delicious treats.

Cassia wanted to open the door and kick the woman, grab the bag, and slam the door shut again. It was way, way, way too early for this.

Moments earlier, Cassia had woken to the sound of banging at the front door. For some reason, Genevieve never seemed to bother with the bell.

Cassia opened the door. Beyond Genevieve, she could see that the sun had barely cleared the trees, and there was still dew on the grass. The morning smelled earthy and damp. This was definitely earlier than she wanted to get up after a late night working a busy fish fry Friday. That inheritance money better come, and soon, because she did not want to be a waitress any longer. It was not her jam, as Genevieve would put it.

"Morning, sunshine," Genevieve said, shoving a cup of coffee into Cassia's hands.

"I have coffee here," Cassia said grumpily.

"And now you have more." Genevieve pushed past Cassia,

nearly knocking her over with the bag that was slung over her shoulder. "Time to get moving. We've got classes to go to."

"I thought you said they were late morning. 11 am is late morning," Cassia mimicked, staring at a nonexistent watch on her wrist. "This is too early o'clock."

"Have a donut. You'll feel better. Sugar solves everything. I got clothes for you and I don't want to be rushed trying to pick out the best outfit."

Cassia groaned. "I've got clothes. Remember that red dress? I'll wear that again. Please, please do not make me wear anything else."

Genevieve frowned, looking unsure for the first time. "I thought you wanted my help."

A pang of guilt shot through Cassia. "Sorry. I do want your help... did want your help, but then I realized I'm not nearly as daring as you are. Wearing your clothes scares me. They're so bold. And skimpy sometimes."

"Only the skirts," Genevieve said, as if that would somehow make it better.

Cassia sucked in her lips.

Genevieve took in Cassia's expression and nodded. "Okay, I see. No problem. I'll wear something from the stash. You wear your red dress."

"Good plan," Cassia said, patting Genevieve on the back and then turning to shut the front door.

———

The gentle rocking of the car in the warm morning sun lulled Cassia to sleep in the passenger seat of Genevieve's car as they drove to Ricardo's dance studio. It was the one benefit about not having her own car, and Cassia was tired enough to take advantage of it and not feel guilty. It wasn't her fault Genevieve had shown up so early, all raring to go.

The route looked much different in the daytime, with the occasional open field full of overgrown grass, but mostly grove after grove of pine trees. The crisp smell of sap filled the air and came in the car through the cracked windows.

Genevieve hummed to herself as she did when she was happy. Cassia had thought the humming strange at first, but after a while she'd stopped noticing it. Now it would've been strange to not hear it. In the sunny fall morning, the strange horribleness of Wednesday night seemed like a dream that never happened, and all was right with the world.

But the world had other plans... and interests.

"Holy freaking buckets," Genevieve said as they crested the last turn of her shortcut through the woods into town.

"What?" Cassia opened her bleary eyes and sat up.

"The town is packed." Genevieve pointed ahead, then pulled the car over to one side so they could check out the view below them without her having to worry about crashing into a tree.

"Is there a festival or something going on?"

"Not that I know of," Genevieve said. She pulled out her phone from her bag and started scrolling through the news. "Oh man, I think I found it."

"What?" Cassia asked again. She leaned in to see Genevieve's phone screen.

"It's a big expose about what happened Wednesday night at the Wild Horses Banquet Hall and the film's connection to Ricardo and the dance studio."

"No way. Weren't we told not to discuss that with anybody?"

Genevieve nodded, then looked from the story on her phone to the crowds of gawkers down below them. "Sheriff Andrews is going to have a fit."

120

CHAPTER 15

The feeling in the crowd in town where the dance studio was located felt different than the first night when Cassia and Genevieve had visited the opening night party. Now, instead of mostly women dressed up in party dresses laughing and giggling and having a good time, more somber faced reporters stood around, their utilitarian gray and black jackets blending into one another, making the group of them look like an ominous cloud. Some had photographers with them, with their enormous cameras and flashes up and facing the door to the studio.

From the outside, the studio looked different, much different. No holiday lights twinkled in the windows to frame a warm and welcoming interior. Instead, black film shades that Cassia didn't even know existed had been pulled down over all the studio's large pane glass windows, causing the mirrored finish of the windows to reflect images of the reporters crowding around the sidewalk back at them.

Rather than being a happy fall morning, this seemed more like a funeral.

As they approached the studio, pushing through the

reporters on the sidewalk, Cassia asked, "Do you think they're still having classes?"

"I hope so," Genevieve said. "If they give in to this, I don't know if their business will make it."

"You mean Ricardo might go back to LA?"

At the word 'Ricardo', several reporters turned to Cassia. One bold one pushed toward her. "Do you know Mr. Ricardo Baros?"

"No," Cassia said. At Genevieve's look, she clarified. "I know of him, but know him? No."

"What do you know of him?" the reporter asked, his eyes gleaming.

Oh boy, now she did it.

"Nothing. I just know he has a dance studio here," Cassia said. She angled to walk around the reporter, but he side-stepped, preventing her from leaving.

"How long has the dance studio been here? What kind of teacher is he? Was Polina Jan-Baros ever in the studio?" the reporter asked, with more questions chiming in from the other reporters around him pressing in toward Cassia and Genevieve.

Cassia's breath caught in her throat. There was not enough air in their little circle, and the reporters were only pushing closer and closer, jostling Genevieve and Cassia into each other.

"No comment," Genevieve called out authoritatively.

"Yeah, no comment," Cassia said, repeating the statement over and over again like a mantra.

The reporters weren't buying it. They refused to move when Cassia and Genevieve tried to walk forward.

The door to the dance studio swung open behind the mass of reporters, and Cassia could see Lucas's steel gray hair above the crowd.

"Let them through," he bellowed, his deep voice cutting through the crowd.

The reporters stopped asking questions and turned en masse to stare at Lucas. They hesitated for one second before they moved toward him and started throwing questions at him. Genevieve grabbed Cassia's wrist and pulled her around the back of the reporters, skirting the crowd and slipping into the dance studio behind Lucas, who had his arms crossed and was glaring at the reporters. He answered just enough questions to keep their attention, Cassia noticed gratefully.

The inside of the studio was dim, with only half of the lights turned on, as if the inhabitants were hiding from the outside world.

Which they were.

And there were a surprising lot of them. There were nearly as many people as there had been on the studio's opening night. Cassia recognized the man with the slicked back hair and his happy smile, which looked slightly dimmed after the day's stress. This time he had on an orange and yellow sweater, also handmade, as if he were trying to personally be the sun and light up the room. The black outfit was gone.

Similarly, the mostly women who were there were dressed in their finery and had on slightly brittle smiles. In the corner, Jane worked at the computer that controlled the sound system and speakers, although no music was playing at the moment.

Ricardo was nowhere to be seen, but then again, last time he had made a dramatic entrance. Maybe he did that every day, or maybe he was just spooked by all the reporters out front.

Even with the door shut, the sounds of shouted questions and Lucas's rumbling answers leaked in through the front glass.

No one in the studio spoke. Cassia doubted anyone outside could hear them talking, but that didn't seem to reassure anyone inside.

"Well, this is a different feel," Genevieve said in Cassia's ear. Cassia had to agree. "Brave group," Genevieve continued. True, but was it even worth trying to carry on, if they were going to be like this?

A moment later, one of the front doors swung open and Lucas entered with a rush of energy. He stood and pointedly pushed the door shut again, instead of letting it leisurely close on its own, then walked to the wall and flipped the rest of the lights on. He clapped his hands. "All right, all right. Shake it off. We're here to have fun."

Lucas stared right at Cassia with a look she could not interpret. Was he happy to see her? Did he remember the other night? She sure hadn't forgotten it.

Breaking their gaze, Lucas walked around to the front of the room and motioned for everyone to line up. Once they had done so, he opened his mouth to give further directions, but was interrupted when Ricardo opened the door from the back and stepped into the room. He wore his customary black tailored clothing, but instead of his usual man bun, his hair was down and flowing around his face in a dramatic black cloud.

There was no other way to put it; Ricardo looked amazing. Like the tragic figure that Cassia always imagined Heathcliff looked like from Wuthering Heights. It had been ages since she'd read that book, but she still remembered the characters, and while the way she cast them probably had little to do with the way the author had described them, that didn't matter. At this point, what mattered was the story in her head.

And Ricardo was the star.

Cassia shook herself.

What was happening? She was a scientist. *A scientist.* Scientists wouldn't get flustered or lovesick over random men. Especially older men.

There must be something in the water here, because there were just way too many good-looking men in this state and it was starting to make Cassia feel like an idiot. And probably act like one too.

When Ricardo entered the studio, the students broke their discipline and walked from their lines to gather around him.

He held up a hand. "No need, no need. Let's focus on dancing," he said, giving the crowd a smile. It looked a little sad and tragic, but was still a smile. Those around him nodded and backed up and went back to the positions slowly, as if making a show of putting a good face on it. No matter how anyone acted, it was hard to shake off being rattled from the crowds of nosy reporters they knew were outside.

The reporters who wanted nothing more than to write some scandalous piece on the studio.

Ricardo paired them off, deciding instead to do a tango, rather than lining them up to learn the steps of some piece individually. Cassia was grateful for the more difficult dance, giving her something to focus on other than what was going on around them.

She lucked out enough to be paired with the man with the yellow and orange sweater. He gave her a brilliant smile, and she couldn't help but respond.

"Quite exciting these days, isn't it?" he asked. She nodded, not wanting to talk about just how exciting it had been. Far too much for her taste.

After demonstrating the steps, Ricardo had the group try out the first few groupings in their pairs. Once he was satisfied, he gave Jane a nod, and music poured through the overhead speakers. Ricardo motioned again, and as a group they started the dance.

It felt amazing.

Much to Cassia's disbelief, she and her dance partner, Mark as it turned out, successfully completed the dance steps without breaking anyone's toes, or even stepping on anyone's feet. It was something Cassia would not of thought possible a week ago. It was rather fun to feel the red dress swirling around her legs as she did the turns. Mark's encouraging smiles and "good jobs" didn't hurt either.

Soon after, they took a break. The students gathered at a back table filled with refreshments that some of the women had been kind enough to bring, and sat to eat them in groups on the studio floor, there being no other seating.

Cassia was relieved more than anything that Ricardo and Lucas were sitting in a different group. As stunning as she found Ricardo's looks, it was difficult to be around him. She doubted she could eat if he was close enough to see her do it. Genevieve seemed to have no such problem and had planted herself right next to Ricardo and was talking to him as if he was her best friend.

Genevieve never failed to amaze Cassia.

One of the women from Cassia's group even went over and brought a plate of rice crispy bars and miniature sandwiches to Jane and asked her to come over and meet them. Jane shyly nodded, accepted the plate, and then came over slowly. A woman in a beautiful purple paisley dress handed her a full glass of lemonade. Jane joined their circle on the floor.

"So how do you like Minnesota?" one of the women asked.

"It's okay. A little cold," Jane answered shyly, mumbling down into her plate instead of looking at the woman she was talking to.

The woman laughed at her answer. "This is warm for this time of year."

Jane shook her head, still looking down, but Cassia could see the creep of red flush along Jane's face and neck.

"I have to agree with Jane," Cassia said with a dramatic huff. "It's way too cold here. I'm from California, and I do *not* like this."

The woman to Cassia's left laughed. "It's because you're way too skinny. You need to eat more, then you won't be so cold. Here, take this," the woman said as she leaned over and dumped a pile of small peanut butter cookies from her plate onto Cassia's. Cassia loved peanut butter cookies, so she didn't even argue, instead just smiling her thanks. A quick glance at Jane showed that the girl appreciated having the focus taken off her and not being the only one who didn't like the cold.

They had just cleared away the paper plates into the large trash bin in the back and dusted the crumbs off their clothing as they lined up to work on the tango again, when a commotion happened outside, loud enough to be heard even over the low music Jane had playing in the background. The shouting increased until something or someone slammed against one of the front windows, causing the black shade in front of the window to vibrate.

Cassia's heart pounded in her chest. The noise was scary enough, but not being able to see what was going on was worse.

Lucas held up one finger for the class to hold back as he and Ricardo went to the door to see what was going on. Just as Ricardo reached for the door to pull it open, it was pushed hard from the outside, sending Ricardo back in a stumble.

Sheriff Andrews and Deputy Chester came in, with Deputy Chester facing backwards and pushing back at the reporters trying to follow him inside. Sheriff Andrews' face was red with agitation, and even normally shy and quiet Deputy Chester was moving faster than normal.

Jane cut the music, and suddenly the questions shouted from the outside reporters floated into the studio. Ricardo and Lucas's names were among the discernible words.

Finally, Deputy Chester managed to push the door shut,

straining to make the air mechanism work faster than it wanted to.

The students and teachers faced Sheriff Andrews and Deputy Chester, each side breathing heavily. Finally, Sheriff Andrews drew himself up, recovering from the gauntlet outside.

"Ricardo Baros," Sheriff Andrews said.

Ricardo stepped forward. "Here," he said, his accent stronger than Cassia had ever heard it.

Sheriff Andrews stepped toward Ricardo, at the same time reaching for the handcuffs on his belt.

"Ricardo Baros, you are under arrest for the murder of Polina Jan-Baros. You have the right to remain silent..."

The roaring in Cassia's head took over and she didn't hear the rest of what Sheriff Andrews said before he led Ricardo out the door and into the crowd of questioning reporters and popping flashes outside.

CHAPTER 16

As Sheriff Andrews and Deputy Chester left with Ricardo, Jane ran to the door and tried to go after them, crying and yelling. "No!" she called. Lucas caught her arm just as she was about to exit and grabbed her and pulled her close. She cried into his chest and beat at him, but he wouldn't let her go.

Students in the studio watched, transfixed, barely breathing. For a few minutes, all that was audible was Jane's crying, muted yells from outside, and the dull drone of the studio's heating unit. Cassia guessed she probably looked like the other students, with shock on their faces and their mouths in small circles of surprise. Most of these students had not been at the Wild Horses Banquet Hall and so had not seen what had happened there. Those that had tried to show up had been turned away by Deputy Chester, who had been posted after Polina's body had been discovered early in the evening.

Some of them had probably even missed the news article that came out this morning.

Gradually, students started talking to each other, their voices kept in low whispers. They clustered together, and a few went to their purses set along the back wall to grab their phones and start scrolling, trying to figure out if something new had been published.

Genevieve walked to Cassia and stood close while looking at Jane and Lucas and the rest of the group inside the building. It now felt oddly empty without Ricardo. "This is not good," Genevieve said.

Cassia nodded, not quite feeling up to talking yet. All she could feel was shock.

Jane yelled something up at Lucas and everyone's heads turned to look at her. Glancing at the staring students, Lucas crouched down to talk to Jane at eye level, and finally convinced her to go into the back. The students parted, leaving a path for Lucas and Jane to make their way to the back door and out. Once the door clicked shut, the volume of the talking in the studio rose considerably.

"Do you think he did it?" Cassia asked, hoping the other students wouldn't hear her under the cacophony of other voices.

"No, of course not," Genevieve said. "But I don't know what we can do about it. Roger no longer has access. Maybe there's something new we don't know about."

Cassia nodded numbly and thought about poor Jane, who might now have lost both parents.

A fate Cassia knew and wouldn't wish upon anybody.

———

"Are you sure you don't want to come in? There's food and stuff." Cassia asked as she leaned to look inside Genevieve's car from the open passenger door. The beautiful sunny morning had turned into a cloudy afternoon, with thick clouds ranging from gray to darker gray where they reached down to the ground, promising late afternoon thunderstorms. The wind blew briskly from behind Cassia, sending cold air up her jacket and throwing her hair around.

Genevieve shook her head. "Not today. I think the lack of sleep is finally getting to me." Her normally sunny disposition looked unusually serious and glum.

"Okay. Call me later," Cassia said, then shut the door and watched as the blue Honda finished pulling around the driveway of the Mandress mansion and drove away toward the nestle of trees that marked the edge of the front lawn.

Cassia stood on the mansion's broad stoop, feeling the oncoming storm. Perhaps she should have tried harder to get Genevieve to stay, but she had to admit to herself that being alone was a bit of a relief. It had been a horrible morning, she was tired, and going back to bed sounded just like the thing for a better day.

At least if she was sleeping, she wouldn't have to think about what Jane looked like when her father was led away.

———

Cassia sat at the kitchen counter with a giant bowl of instant oatmeal filled with nuts, chocolate chips, and raisins. Oatmeal was her comfort food, and these were all the goodies she could find in the pantry. What she really wanted was some maple syrup, but there was none to be had. Miss Mansfield sat on the stool next to her, primly washing her paw and face. Usually the cat would wander off after breakfast or lunch, but this time, perhaps knowing that Cassia was upset, she hung around the kitchen. Maybe Miss Mansfield cared about her after all, but she wasn't above pretending she was just there to clean herself and that Cassia just happened to be in the same room. Cassia snorted. That was okay. She knew lots of people like that.

Finishing half the bowl, Cassia sighed, put her spoon down

and pushed the rest away. Her stomach was full, but she still didn't feel any better. Outside, thunder rumbled in the distance. The storm had been coming for half an hour and was finally getting close enough for the flashes of lightning to be seen inside the mansion, even with the lights on in the late afternoon.

Getting up from her stool, Cassia went over to the counter where the picture of Richard Nixon lay against the wall. Picking it up, she checked the back again. The inscription in blue ink read:

V.P.N., 1957

If what Genevieve said was true, then the N probably stood for Nixon. But what about the V and the P? Cassia pulled out her phone and decided it was worth splurging on some data to figure this out. After a few searches, and reading about his history, it clicked with her that VP must stand for Vice President. He was Vice President Nixon in 1957.

Which meant it was a really big deal that he had come to the mansion at that time.

Why?

It looked like he had been out in the telescope dome. Perhaps it had something to do with that. More Internet searches revealed a biography page dedicated to him. Apparently he had been a big proponent of space travel, pushing then President Eisenhower to create the civilian organization NASA.

NASA?

Holy cow, her relatives had something to do with NASA?

Stunned, Cassia put down her phone. If she hadn't witnessed such horrible events this morning, she would have been ecstatic at this point. Now she just felt confused. Would it be too much to ask the universe to just give her some good things for a while, and not always sprinkle them with some terrible events as well?

Suddenly she missed her parents with a fierce longing she

hadn't felt in a long time. Or to have any relatives. To have known Mildred Mandress while she was still alive, or Senior Mandress. Just knowing that he had had an interest in astronomy made Cassia feel better. Neither of her parents had, not that she had known them all that well before they died, and she felt a little bit of a freak to have such a strong interest seemingly out of nowhere.

Pushing away from the island, Cassia got up and grabbed the large ring of house keys from the hook where they hung inside the cabinet just to the left of the refrigerator. The thing was massive, and she had long ago taken the key to the front door off of it, but now she needed access to a room she hadn't gone into for a month.

Climbing the stairs to the second floor, Cassia marveled once again at the enormous size of the house. There were two full wings, one coming off to the right and one to the left of the main landing above the front entryway. It looked like something out of a nighttime soap opera, where imaginary rich people lived in imaginary huge houses, except this house was real, and so was Cassia.

Padding next to her, Miss Mansfield kept up with her tiny black paws. She gave a soft little meow, as if to remind Cassia she was there, but was otherwise silent as she walked next to her. Cassia took a right turn at the top of the second floor landing. The doors on the ride side of the hallway were all still shut, and the rooms inside of them still unused, the heavy furniture within covered with dusty sheets. Someday she was going to have enough money to pay people to open up these rooms and clean them.

Someday she was going to have the belongings that were once within them.

All she needed was a bit more money.

It was always the money.

There were no doors on the left side of the hallway,

133

because that was where the two-story library was. At least Cassia had that. The thought cheered her up a bit.

At the end of the hallway, Cassia turned right to another set of stairs that rose, twisting about with several landings to the third floor.

The amazing third floor that Cassia guessed had been her aunt's bedroom.

Cassia climbed the stairs until she reached the double doors of the third-floor landing. Even the entryway was decorated with outlandishly fancy painted white carved molding over a beautiful light blue paint job.

Only the beautiful lacquered doors stood free of paint, their only decoration instead the beautiful deep shine of the highly polished wood, looking like two enormous pieces of amber.

Cassia pulled two skeletons keys from her ring and fitted them in the double lock below the door handles and turned them in unison, releasing the mechanism. The doors swung gently open, revealing the excesses and beauty inside.

In the dim light, both from the dark skies outside, and from the heavy curtains pulled across the windows, Cassia could make out the shapes of the four-poster bed that itself was large enough to contain her old apartment living room, as well as the various seating areas placed around the room. Dressers and bureaus and desks filled out the rest of the space.

This room encompassed the entire third floor of the mansion, so to say it was large was understating it. It resembled a football field with furniture.

Cassia opened some of the curtains to reveal the gray sky outside. The trees outside waved and struggled in the intense wind. Suddenly, a spate of rain hit the window Cassia stood in front of, making her jump back with her heart racing.

Then the rain came down in a torrent, washing over the window in mesmerizing grayish-green waves.

Walking to the enormous bed, Cassia climbed on top and pulled one of the pillows close, ignoring the faint musty smell. Miss Mansfield jumped up next to her and curled in a circle, keeping her little kitty back pressed up against Cassia's waist. The warmth felt nice.

Cassia rested her other hand on her chest and soon fell asleep.

Cassia floated in outer space. The Earth hung in the sky, a distant green and blue marble, much the same size as a full moon.

Despite not being on Earth, Cassia didn't feel any panic, at least not until the asteroids started coming at her. Black, craggy rocks with mist trailing after them whizzed by her head. The fact that she should not be able to hear anything in space, much less the whizzing of asteroids, preoccupied her thoughts, until another asteroid came directly at her, forcing her to bend down and try to get her enormous space-helmeted head out of the way. Since there was nothing to push on or off of, she didn't go anywhere, instead wiggling in space like a worm on a sidewalk after a heavy rain.

"Oh crap," Cassia said, as the asteroid hit her directly in the chest. Instead of slamming into her like she expected the enormous rock to do, it gently pressed on her in a rhythmic pattern. Push, push, push. It also beeped.

The asteroid beeped?

Forcing herself awake, Cassia opened her eyes, sleep clogging her eyelashes. It was dark, so dark that she reached up to feel her eyes to make sure they were open. Her hand brushed against warm fur.

Miss Mansfield sat on her chest, kneading her paws in. The

tiny cat felt a lot larger when she was sitting directly on Cassia's diaphragm.

"What are you doing?" Cassia asked groggily.

The cat gave a soft meow and then jumped off Cassia to walk next to her on the bed. Cassia rolled over and saw her phone laying next to her with its screen lit up. It was also beeping. *Beep, beep.*

Someone was texting her, repeatedly. Picking up the phone she looked at the messages. Genevieve had texted her five times. It looked like she had a bunch of missed calls as well.

"Oh no," Cassia muttered as she sat up.

She opened one of the messages. *"Jane ran away. Call me!"*

Cassia glanced at the window. It was full dark out, and the wind still howled.

"No, no, no," Cassia muttered. She slid to the edge of the bed and got off while pressing the button to call Genevieve back.

CHAPTER 17

The rain had stopped for a while, but was now pouring down again, lashing against the mansion and running in a small river across the turnabout in front of the front door. The temperature had dropped at least thirty degrees from the warm midday and felt closer to winter. Cassia leaned out into the rain and peered down the driveway. No headlights yet. She quickly retreated back into the house and shut the door.

Standing inside the entryway, Miss Mansfield sat and stared at her.

"Yes, I know I'm crazy," Cassia muttered to the cat.

Maybe she had something warmer to wear. Cassia hadn't realized how cold it was outside now. Running back to the room she claimed as her bedroom in the back of the house, Cassia flung open the door and then dug into some of the moving boxes still packed with clothing from her trip out from California. She found another light sweater and a black bucket hat. She didn't care how silly the hat looked, as long as it was as warm.

Pulling off her raincoat, Cassia tugged on the sweater over her shirt, shoved the hat on her head, and grabbed her raincoat to go back and keep watch at the front door. Even as she was approaching the door she could see Genevieve's headlights through the front glass.

Exiting the mansion, Cassia turned and struggled with the lock, feeling rainwater go down the back of her neck. Yet another thing to fix when she had money.

She ran to the car and opened the door, grateful Genevieve had positioned the passenger door closest to the mansion. Even so, she was sopping wet by the time she got into the car and slammed the door shut.

"What happened?" Cassia asked in a rush. "And how did you know?" These are the questions she'd been dying to ask Genevieve on the first call, but didn't dare delay Genevieve from getting in the car and driving over to pick her up.

"An alert went out to all the business owners in the neighboring towns. They asked people to close early and have their employees help with the search. It's also on the news. I don't suppose you watched that?" Genevieve asked.

Cassia shook her head. "No TV."

Genevieve glanced over. "Your phone?"

"True," Cassia said. "But I was asleep. Did they send out a text alert?"

Genevieve shrugged. She was uncharacteristically leaning forward in her seat, peering out the front windshield while driving. The rain was coming down so heavily it was hard to see anything, and Genevieve kept the car to a slow crawl.

"Each town is sending out a group. I told Trent we were going down to the dance studio to meet up with that town's group. It's probably closer to where she is anyhow. He thought that'd be fine. He can deal with Sheriff Andrews for once."

Good idea. Cassia was still upset by the whole day's events. Sheriff Andrews was just doing his job, but she couldn't help but be a little upset at how badly Jane took it.

The drive over seemed to take forever. Water flooded the road, and it felt in some places like the car floated and slid more than it drove forward. Cassia turned up the heat and had all the air vents blasting hot air on only herself. Genevieve didn't want it so warm. It interfered with her concentration.

Cassia rubbed her hands and held them in front of the heater. If she was this cold from just running out to the car from the mansion, then Jane was in a lot of trouble if she'd been out there in all that mess for long. Of all the nights to run away, this must be one of the worst ones to pick.

"Do they have any idea where she might have gone?" Cassia asked. "Did Trent say anything?"

"No, not much information. Just that she's been gone for several hours, and the local sheriff is quite irate that Lucas took so long to report her missing."

"Don't they usually need like a twenty-four-hour absence or something like that?" Cassia asked. Not that she wanted to wait a day to look for the girl, she was just surprised.

"I think so, but with everything that happened with her father, and the storm, the sheriff thought... well, I don't think any of them have an appetite for a young girl to die on their watch."

No, that would not be good.

By the time they got to the dance studio, the rain had stopped, and the streets shone slickly black under the street-lights. Cassia checked the time on her phone. 1 am. It was already Sunday. That storm had gone on for hours, and if Jane had been out in it... She didn't want to finish that thought.

Running up to the studio, they found a lone female deputy waiting for them.

"Where is everyone?" Genevieve asked.

"They're already out there," the deputy explained. "They

went out as soon as there was a lull in the rain. We might be in luck."

Cassia looked at the deputy questioningly.

The deputy pointed up.

Cassia looked up and saw the constellation of Orion's Belt twinkling above her. Not only had the rain stopped, but the clouds were starting to blow away. With any luck, the disappearing clouds would reveal a moon to give them more light.

"Thanks for waiting for us," Genevieve said.

"Policy," the deputy said gruffly, though softening it with a smile. "No one searches alone. We don't need two tragedies."

"I hope there's not even one," Cassia said under her breath. She must have said it louder than she intended, because both the deputy and Genevieve looked at her and then nodded.

———

"So, where are we going?" Genevieve asked. She leaned forward and stared at all the strange buttons and gizmos on the deputy's dashboard. She reached out a finger to touch something but the deputy put out a blocking hand without even looking. It was the instinctive action of someone who either had kids or younger siblings. Genevieve sighed dramatically but retracted her finger and leaned back into the passenger seat of the deputy's cruiser.

Cassia watch from the backseat, somewhat enjoying the ride behind the thick plastic divider. She wasn't in trouble on this ride, which made it somewhat amusing and not terrifying.

Deputy Katelin Porter worked for Bellard County, which is why they'd seen her at the Wild Horses Banquet Hall. She'd been the lone female deputy that night when Polina had been found.

The sky had cleared up completely in the few moments it

had taken them to get to the deputy's cruiser and hop in. The search group had divided up the area ahead of time, and Deputy Porter had the coordinates of their assigned section.

"We're heading just west and north of town. Back toward where you guys came from, actually. It's pretty far from the house the Baroses had rented, and even further from her grandfather's house, but our sheriff likes to be thorough. Have to go through every section."

"Sounds like a good plan," Genevieve said, nodding her agreement. Cassia was content to let Genevieve do the talking for both of them. It was too much work to shout forward from the backseat.

After about twenty minutes, the deputy pulled over to the side of a dark road, the vehicle tilting dangerously to one side because of the steep shoulder. They didn't bother to make these roads any wider than they had to be.

Genevieve and Deputy Porter got out of the car. Cassia realized with dismay there was no way to open her door herself. She had to wait for Deputy Porter to come back and open the back door. Cassia pushed down the momentary panic she felt while trapped inside the vehicle. Genevieve was going to ride in back on the way home. It suddenly didn't seem so fun anymore.

The deputy had parked her car in the central area of two large fields spreading on either side of the road. The quarter moon that had come out shone down on the fields, giving them a silvery light. Beyond the fields in all directions lay a ring of woods, dark with black shadows. The fields were fine. Unfortunately, it was probably the woods where they would have any luck finding the girl, and they were definitely the scariest part of the scenery.

"We're sticking together in this search, right?" Cassia asked Deputy Porter and Genevieve, trying to come off as nonchalant as Deputy Porter handed out flashlights from the trunk of her car.

Cassia had not really understood what "comb" had meant when Deputy Porter had said it. Well, she thought she did, but an hour later, two sore feet, and loads of mud told her otherwise. They had methodically walked the fields on both sides, keeping the three of them within finger touching distance of each other so if there was anything or anybody laying in the fields, they would not miss them.

Those fields had not escaped the rain from earlier, so it didn't take more than one pass through the first field before Cassia's sneakers were completely soaked, and each step sent fresh water shooting between her toes and out the sneakers. Or mud. Cassia could swear she could feel grains of mud between her toes that had to have come in through the sneaker vents, or over the top of her socks.

However the mud and water had come in, it was there now, and Cassia had never wanted anything so much as she wanted to take those sneakers and throw them away deep into the woods, and then crawl into a hot warm bath, but she bit her lip and said nothing. She was fussing in her mind because her feet were cold and wet, but she had not been out here when it had been raining sheets of water. She was not a young girl who had lost both her mother and probably her father.

So Cassia was not going to complain, not tonight.

Instead, the three of them kept walking through the fields, scanning the high grasses for any evidence that Jane had been here.

After completing the fields, they went back to the cruiser to take a break and stretch. Deputy Porter popped the trunk and pulled out three bottles of water, sharing one each with Cassia and Genevieve. Gratefully, Cassia twisted off the top and drank half a bottle. Vaguely, she thought she should ration it, but she was too thirsty to care.

"Now the woods," Deputy Porter said, screwing the cap back on her bottle and tossing it into the trunk. She waited until Cassia and Genevieve deposited their own bottles back in the trunk and slammed the lid. The sound of the trunk shutting sent strange echoes bouncing back from the trees in the distance. The echoes gave Cassia a shiver, as if the woods were talking to them, and not in the kindest way.

Pushing her fears down, Cassia walked between Deputy Porter and Genevieve as they headed toward the closest edge of the woods.

"Should we be calling for her?" Cassia asked.

"We can," said Deputy Porter. "Actually we should, but we have to be careful because we also want to be quiet enough to hear her respond if she does call out. That's the problem if too many people yell at once."

"Got it," Genevieve said. She raised her wrist with her watch and fiddled with it for a few minutes. "How about once a minute, or every two minutes…?"

"Two minutes," Deputy Porter said.

"Done," Genevieve said, pressing the side button on her watch. Then she leaned back and cupped her hand with her mouth and yelled out, "Jane!"

The three of them stood, silently listening for any response. Nothing, then the faint hoot of a distant owl.

Genevieve shrugged. They walked on to the edge of the woods.

The moonlight penetrated the woods a short distance, making them seem a little less terrifying up close. Cassia clenched and unclenched her hands to try to get herself to relax. She was with other people. There was nothing to fear in the woods.

As if the woods were mocking her by placing a trap, Cassia stepped on a large branch that snapped with a loud crack and dropped her several inches to the moist ground below it. She managed to not scream, but she did double over and put a hand on her racing heart.

"You okay?" Genevieve asked Cassia, all her normal teasing gone.

Cassia nodded. She appreciated Genevieve's sincerity. She didn't have the extra energy to deal with teasing at the moment.

They continued their technique of pacing through the woods, more challenging than the fields with the extra bonus of having to avoid the trees, but there was less undergrowth and they could see the ground better.

At one point Cassia thought she heard a voice that sounded exactly like a man's deep voice, and she made Genevieve and Deputy Porter stop, but when they heard it again, Deputy Porter laughed and only said, "That's a frog." Cassia was glad the darkness hid her blush.

To keep from getting lost in the woods, Deputy Porter had been counting their paces and insisting they only go two hundred paces into the woods before turning around and coming back. They could do the woods more thoroughly in the daylight hours when they had the sun to help them. The sky to the east was already turning pink. Daylight was not far away now anyhow.

On their last venture into the woods, Cassia thought she saw a length of yellow fabric hanging from a tree branch ahead of them, but it was hard to tell.

"Turn," Deputy Porter called.

"Wait, I think I see something," Cassia said, pointing.

"Okay, we'll head over there—" Deputy Porter said, but was cut short by Cassia rushing ahead. "No, stop! Don't run!" Deputy Porter called.

Genevieve tried to grab Cassia's wrist but missed. "Wait for us!"

But Cassia didn't hear them until she'd run to the branch

and realized two things: it was just an old rag that looked newer in the moonlight, and second, the woods hid a steep drop-off on the other side of the bushes and she had just gone too far.

Cassia screamed as she slid down the side of the ravine.

CHAPTER 18

The bright half moon shone down on the thickly vegetated ravine. Raindrops from the earlier storm still hung from some branches. Dead and falling leaves filled the space between the twiggy branches of the bare trees that were interspersed between the craggy pines.

Through the middle of the hillside, a slick path of mud glimmered in a straight path from the top of the ravine to the bottom, ending in a pile of dead leaves and twigs.

The pile of dead leaves vibrated for moment and then settled again.

After the abrupt yelling and shouting of the past few minutes, the silence that settled over the ravine calmed its inhabitants like a blanket. Finally, a frog, emboldened by the quiet, let out a call, soon matched by his friends.

Cassia, dazed and disoriented within the pile of leaves, slowly righted herself and sat up. Leaves fell off her head as she rose from the pile. Her whole body ached. She moved slowly, afraid to find something broken. Nothing seemed to be.

The frogs only called louder, as if mocking her and her clumsiness.

"Oh shut up," Cassia said, her terror receding, only to be replaced by crabby tiredness.

"Cat? Cassia!" a voice called from above.

"Gen," Cassia called back. Or tried to. It came out more like a croak. Cassia coughed, then tried again. "Gen. Genevieve!"

"Stay there," Genevieve yelled back. "We'll come to get you."

"Don't come the way I did," Cassia said, not bothering to yell that response.

She examined her clothing. They were covered in dirt, and her rain jacket was ripped from the right armpit all the way to the back. Great. By some miracle, her bucket hat was still jammed on her head, although one of her soggy shoes was missing. How did that happen? She lifted her leg and wiggled her now gray sock in the moonlight. If she wasn't so cold, she would have ripped the sock off and tossed it deep into the woods. She was really sick of being wet and cold.

Moving slowly like an old lady, Cassia struggled to her feet, or rather her foot, trying to keep most of her weight on the foot that still had a shoe. She peered up the hillside, trying to see if she could spot her other shoe. It might be that white blotch three quarters of the way up the hill, which meant it might as well be on the moon. She wasn't going back up the hill that way, and it was doubtful that Genevieve and Deputy Porter would come down that way either.

———

It probably only took Deputy Porter and Genevieve thirty minutes to find a way down the hillside to Cassia, even though it felt to Cassia like hours. She had finally given up on standing, and had instead just sat down on the wet ground and glumly felt the moisture soak into her pants. She was too tired to even care. As long as she got a bath when she got home, all would be well.

Deputy Porter and Genevieve's quick time was even more impressive because they had gone back to the car and retrieved a much larger flashlight unit, giving out almost as much light as a spotlight. It looked like it weighed about twenty pounds, and even in the dim light Cassia could see the sweat on Deputy Porter's brow from carrying it down the side of the ravine. Cassia had watched their progress down the hill further to her left, where the slope looked more gentle. It had been like watching a small sun progress down through the trees.

"How come you didn't use that while we were doing the searching?" Cassia asked by way of greeting, pointing to the enormous light, then turning away to shield her eyes until Deputy Porter turned off the super intense beam.

"Heavy," Deputy Porter said. "Although maybe I should have."

Cassia bit her lip to refrain from saying anything sarcastic. It was clearly her own fault for falling down the hill, and she knew it, so there was no sense in griping about the lack of light. She should not have rushed ahead, and that was all there was to it.

"You guys didn't happen to find my shoe, did you?" Cassia asked.

"Nope, sorry," Genevieve said, looking down at Cassia's unshod foot. "That's gotta suck."

"Yup," Cassia said.

Deputy Porter scanned the hillside and surrounding area before turning back to Genevieve and Cassia. "I think we should give it a rest for now. We can reconvene later in the daylight. Full light is only a few hours away anyhow. Plus, they might have another update meeting."

Cassia and Genevieve nodded. Cassia was glad for the decision, and even more glad she wasn't the one to have to say it. Now she would just have to see if she could find any more tennis shoes in her packed boxes.

They backtracked to the path Genevieve and Deputy Porter took down the hill and slowly made their way back up.

———

Due to Cassia's now filthy nature, she was not able to actually, in fact, ride in the passenger seat of the deputy's car on the way back to the studio. Again she sat in the back, now fully aware that she was locked in, and banished there because she was, to put it mildly, a little muddy.

However, things got better once they got back to Genevieve's car. Cassia had never appreciated Genevieve's tendency to prep for all situations as much as she did this moment when she peeled off her wet socks and pants and dropped them into a plastic bag supplied by Genevieve, and then pulled on warm and clean oversized men's crew socks, and a gigantic set of overalls. She was swimming in them, but she didn't care. They were crisp and clean and warm, and most importantly, dry. She never appreciated dry clothes so much as she did this moment.

Cassia curled up in the passenger seat, pulling her legs and feet up, while Genevieve twisted the plastic bag shut, rolling it into a tight ball, and then tucking it in the backseat before getting in the driver side.

"I'm flipping exhausted," Genevieve said as she turned over the engine.

"Are you okay to drive?" Cassia asked, concerned.

Genevieve shrugged, then turned to scan the backseat. She leaned back and dug in some bags on the floor behind Cassia and pulled out a can of soda. At Cassia's look, she held it up. "Want one?"

Cassia shook her head. The last thing she needed was a

bunch of sugar.

"Okay," Genevieve said. She popped the top to the soda, took a long swig and then put it in the drink holder between the two of them.

Sunrise was definitely coming. While it was still dark to the west, the east was getting a lighter and lighter pink, almost orange. Cassia yawned.

The hypnotic motion of the car cruising the back roads had almost put Cassia to sleep when Genevieve slammed on the brakes, jolting Cassia against the seatbelt.

"What?" Cassia asked, blearily looking around.

"Ahead, and to the right," Genevieve said as she moved the car to the shoulder of the road, then pulled on the parking brake and killed the engine. Genevieve's seatbelt was off and she was out the door before Cassia could even focus on what Genevieve had been talking about.

A motion by the tree line next to the road caught Cassia's eye. In the early morning light, it could have been anything, but then Cassia spied a pigtail flapping as the girl turned to bolt back into the woods.

"Jane," Genevieve called. "Jane!"

The girl hesitated and looked back. Even from a distance, Cassia could see the fear in her face.

Cassia scrambled to get out of the car and join Genevieve.

"Everyone's worried about you," Cassia said.

That was the wrong thing to say. Jane bolted into the woods.

Genevieve ran after her, bounding through the tall grasses and putting on more speed than Cassia had realized she could do.

Grimacing, Cassia looked down at her sock clad feet. There was no use for it. She ran after the two of them, not making as good time as she forced herself not to think about what she might be stepping on.

Cassia made it as far as the tree line when she heard a scramble within the woods. It sounded like Genevieve had tackled the girl, a thought bolstered by the yells coming from within the trees.

Slowing down, Cassia waited for a moment, trying to figure out where they had gone by the sounds. Before she had to make a decision, Genevieve came around a tree with her arm around Jane's neck, dragging the girl along. The girl looked irate and beat on Genevieve's back with her hands, yelling and trying to kick at Genevieve's legs. Genevieve just looked forward and continued to march on, ignoring the girl's struggles as if she was a horsefly bothering Genevieve.

"Genevieve," Cassia said, slightly shocked.

"I guess you've never had younger siblings," Genevieve said to Cassia.

Cassia shook her head slowly, getting a glimpse of a world she would never know.

"I'm not going back!" Jane yelled to the ground, forced to look there by her position under Genevieve's arm.

"Everyone's worried about you," Cassia said, repeating herself.

"Not everyone! I'm not going back. You can't make me," Jane said, trying to kick Genevieve once again. Genevieve neatly moved her knees out of the way, sending Jane off-balance. Jane yelled her rage, her fists clenched.

Genevieve just gave Cassia a bored look. Cassia was astounded. And impressed.

"We've been up all night looking for you, and this one here," Genevieve said, nodding at Cassia, "nearly broke her neck falling down a hill to get you. We're going to keep you safe, whether you want it or not."

"I can't go back!" Jane yelled, and much to Genevieve and Cassia's shock, she started to bawl.

CHAPTER 19

The sun finally made it over the horizon, shining its slanting rays on Genevieve's car still parked by the side of the road, now with both front doors open.

Birds sang and cawed raucously in the early morning light, determined to make sure everyone else was awake too.

Jane sat in the passenger seat of Genevieve's car, a towel around her shoulders and a barely sipped can of soda in her hands. She was no longer bawling, but she still hiccuped from crying, and her eyes were red and puffy. Cassia crouched in front of the girl, drying off Jane's feet with another of Genevieve's towels and putting yet more of Genevieve's clean socks on the girl's feet. Cassia was never going to hassle Genevieve about the packed state of her car ever again.

"I don't want to go," Jane said, for about the thirtieth time.

"We can get in a lot of trouble for not bringing you to safety," Genevieve said, leaning to speak softly to Jane from her position at the side of the car.

"I don't mean to get you in trouble..." Jane said, her face screwing up as if she was going to start bawling again.

"No, no…" Cassia said, patting Jane on the knee. "Don't cry." Cassia looked up at Genevieve and gave her a "stop talking" look. Genevieve might know how to handle younger siblings, but this was different. They had no authority over Jane, and if Jane ran away from them, all they could do was call the sheriff, and then they would be right back where they started.

"How about this?" Cassia said, standing and looking over the landscape as she thought. "How about you come back with us to my place, and get dry, maybe have a shower, or a bath, whatever you want, and eat a big huge feast of a breakfast. We don't have to call the sheriff right away. We can get you cleaned up and fed and come up with a plan that keeps you safe. We will absolutely not turn you over to someone who puts you in danger."

Cassia looked back to Jane, trying to judge how well her words were working. Maybe a little, going by the tentative look Jane gave her. The girl looked absolutely terrible. She was even muddier than Cassia had been after falling down the hill, and her hair was knotted and coming loose of her ponytail.

Despite Cassia's warning glare, Genevieve leaned in again. "Who are you afraid of?"

Jane just stared at Genevieve and bit her lip.

"Your father?" Genevieve asked.

"No!" Jane yelled, and then did start crying again. "My father would never hurt anyone!" she said through her tears.

Cassia crouched down and grabbed Jane in a hug. "It's okay. It's okay. We're sorry. We don't know, so we have to ask… Can you understand that?"

After a few moments of being squeezed by Cassia, Jane calmed down and the tears stopped. She nodded to Cassia's questions. "Yes, I can understand," she said through her sniffles as she pulled back from the embrace.

"How about," Cassia said, looking up meaningfully at Genevieve, "we go to my place and focus on the immediate needs like warm, clean clothes and food. We can negotiate everything else once we're there. And we can't," Cassia raised her eyebrows at Genevieve, "make you stay, but if you go from there at least you'll have had some food and sleep."

Jane looked down, thinking about it.

"What is your favorite food?" Cassia asked, nudging Jane's knee.

"Pancakes," Jane said shyly.

"Pancakes it is, although Genevieve's got to go out and get some maple syrup because I'm all out."

"I'm going to what—" Genevieve started to say, then shut her mouth abruptly as Cassia rose and stepped on Genevieve's toes, leaning in to make sure the subtle motion was effective.

Genevieve made a choking sound.

Moments later, Cassia once again found herself crammed into the backseat of a car and they were off on their way to the Mandress mansion.

———

Morning sun streamed through the back kitchen window, giving some welcome light to the vast space. The normally pristine room looked like a tornado had torn through it. Almost all the cupboards were open. And half the pantry was spread around the floor in front of it.

Miss Mansfield lay curled on her bed on the back desk, her chin on her tail, and her golden eyes watching Cassia dig in the pantry and put yet more cans on the island counter.

Cassia paused what she was doing and stared at the cat. "You could help," Cassia said.

Miss Mansfield answered by stretching her paws forward and then closing her eyes in a slow blink.

It was just as well. It had taken Cassia nearly half an hour to calm down the animal, who was more than a little irate at both missing a second dinner the previous night when Cassia had run out, as well as being second fiddle when Cassia arrived home that morning. After getting Jane settled in the bathroom, Cassia had come back to the kitchen and put out two dishes of food, just to try to be extra nice by laying out a variety for the feline, as well as trying to sweet talk Miss Mansfield the best she could. She'd felt ridiculous, but it had worked, sort of.

At least the angry meows had stopped.

Wiping her brow, Cassia let herself feel all the frustration of the last twenty-four hours for just a moment.

After the moment passed, she took a deep breath and looked around the mess she had made.

"And I thought Sarah had done a good job of stocking this place," she muttered.

She was mostly done putting everything back by the time the front door opened and Genevieve strode down the long hallway to the kitchen.

"Got everything," Genevieve said. "I don't understand how this place didn't have pancake mix." She put down a large paper bag on the kitchen counter.

"Agreed," Cassia said.

"Where's our little prisoner?" Genevieve asked.

Cassia turned to face Genevieve and put her hand on her hip. "Don't say that, not even in jest. We gotta find a way for her to stay here until something better can be done. I don't want her to run off because she's afraid of us."

"Okay, okay. You got a point. No more jokes until we all feel better."

"Deal." Cassia went to the island and grabbed the bag that Genevieve had brought in. Ah-ha, maple syrup. Something for both her and Jane to be happy about. "She's still in the bath, I think."

"Which one?"

Which one what? Puzzled, Cassia turned to Genevieve, then it occurred to her. "My bath. Off my room. I also laid some clothes out for her."

Genevieve snorted. "I should've gone home and got her some clothes too."

"My clothes are not that bad." Cassia didn't turn around to see what face Genevieve was making.

By the time Jane appeared at the kitchen door, swaddled in an enormous blue sweater and brown corduroy pants pulled deep from one of Cassia's packing boxes, the pancakes were made and the table set, complete with orange juice, sausages, syrup and butter. It was the first real homemade meal Cassia had had in the mansion. Most everything else had been frozen dinners or sandwiches.

Jane looked much better. Her dirty ponytail was gone, as well as the grime on her face. She'd washed her hair and combed it back, letting it fall over the shoulders of the sweater. She looked much better in the outfit than Cassia ever had, Cassia noted somewhat grumpily. She should just give the girl the clothes.

"How was the bubble bath?" Cassia asked.

"Great," Jane answered, shyly.

"Come eat," Genevieve said. She pulled out a chair for Jane and motioned to the table. Jane approached and took her chair, only occasionally glancing up at Cassia and Genevieve. Her eyes were mostly down, but also on the food spread out in front of her.

Cassia and Genevieve took their seats next to Jane.

Jane sat quietly with her hands on her lap.

"Is everything okay?" Cassia asked.

Jane nodded.

"You can start. Here, let me help you," Cassia said, picking up the plate holding an enormous stack of pancakes and slid four over onto Jane's plate. The girl's eyes went wide. For the first time in her life, Cassia was starting to understand the joy of feeding someone else. This could be addicting.

Sausages and orange juice, syrup and butter came next.

Soon they were all digging in, only the sound of forks clinking on plates echoing in the kitchen.

Much to Cassia's surprise, Miss Mansfield jumped down from her bed on the desk to come and circle around Jane's chair, rubbing her cheek against the girl's shins and meowing a delicate little welcoming meow. Cassia could not remember ever hearing that sound from Miss Mansfield before. A strange feeling tickled Cassia's chest.

Was that jealousy?

Cassia shook her head, trying to get rid of the silly emotion and earning a curious look from Genevieve, but she waved it away. "Just tired right now." There was no way she was going to admit that she was jealous of the attention of a seven-pound cat.

———

They were mostly done eating, just pushing around the pancakes they couldn't finish on their plates, when the front doorbell rang. Jane looked up, her eyes wide.

Cassia patted her on the shoulder. "Don't worry, I'm sure it's nothing," she said as she rose and set her napkin on the chair before going to answer the door.

Checking out the peephole, she saw Sheriff Andrews' blue eyes looking back at her, his expression a mixture of his normal irate crabbiness and a furrow of concern between his eyebrows.

Cassia slipped out the front door, forcing Sheriff Andrews to step back, and pulled the door shut behind her.

"If she's here, I have to see her," he said, motioning to the door.

Cassia grimaced, motioning for him to step away from the front door so they could talk on the front lawn and their voices not carry as far.

"Her grandfather is demanding to see her," Sheriff Andrews said. "He is her closest kin."

Besides her father, Cassia thought, but didn't bother pointing that out to the man. "Yeah, about that... Did Genevieve explain the situation?" Cassia asked instead.

"Not much. Something about Jane being terrified and not feeling safe at home?"

"Yes," Cassia said. "If she had been stronger, she probably would've beat us up to run away again. I don't think I could've caught her."

Now Sheriff Andrews looked really concerned. "You don't have her tied up in there, do you?"

Cassia crossed her arms. "Of course not. She's eating pancakes."

Sheriff Andrews pushed his hat back and looked around. "If she's really scared, we can call child services, but I don't know how soon they can get out here on a Sunday."

"Can she just stay with us for a day or two? At the mansion?"

Sheriff Andrews must have been really tired, because instead of his normal fire and belligerence, he just looked exhausted as he considered her words.

Cassia almost felt bad for him.

Almost.

The radio at his waist beeped. He pulled it off his belt and checked the screen. "Just a moment," he said to Cassia as he walked back to his cruiser and out of her earshot.

A moment later, Sheriff Andrews returned, all reasonableness gone from his expression. "That was the Bellard Sheriff's Department. They are demanding access to Jane immediately."

Cassia blanched.

CHAPTER 20

Cassia, Genevieve, and Sheriff Andrews all stood around the kitchen table facing Jane. The remains of the breakfast feast were still spread out on the counter, and Cassia and Genevieve's empty dishes were still at their places. Miss Mansfield had taken advantage of Cassia's absence to jump up and sit on the chair next to Jane, and sat on it facing the three adults as if she were Jane's personal guard cat.

Cassia had to give Jane credit. Despite looking terrified with her rounded eyes, Jane sat in the chair and faced the three of them. She wasn't so sure she could have done the same in Jane's position. She probably would've bolted, but then again, Genevieve had proved that wasn't the greatest strategy either.

"Sheriff Andrews has told us that you cannot stay here, for some state reasons I don't understand, honestly," Cassia said. "But if you go down to his office, he and Deputy Chester will guard you until the people from child services come to get you. You don't have to go home."

Jane's mouth quivered in a frown. "What does that mean? Will I never see my dad again?"

"Not necessarily," Sheriff Andrews said. "They just want to

160

talk to you. No one should go somewhere where they're not safe. Is it something with your grandfather?"

Jane shook her head. "I can't tell you. I can't tell you anything." She started to shake, her hand jostling her fork on her plate and making a horrible noise. Suddenly, she pushed her chair away from the table and looked ready to run. Genevieve ran one way around the table, but Cassia beat her going the other way. Cassia knelt at Jane's side and grabbed her hands.

"It's just for a few hours," Cassia said, hoping that was true. At least Sheriff Andrews had promised to only release Jane to the custody of the child services people, and not to the other sheriff's department or to her grandfather. Maybe it would be enough time to try to figure out what was going on.

"Promise me you won't force me back to the house?" Jane asked, sticking out her chin and showing some unexpected spirit. She was looking directly at Sheriff Andrews. He looked unaccustomedly uncomfortable with the direct charge, but did finally say, "I promise."

"Okay," Jane said. "If you come with me," she said to Cassia.

Surprised, Cassia glanced at Sheriff Andrews. He nodded.

"Okay," Cassia said. "But only if I get to have a shower first." While she had a chance to change, and her clothes were no longer muddy, she still felt grimy, as if she could feel dirt ground into every pore of her face and exposed skin.

Sheriff Andrews sighed heavily, but nodded agreement.

———

Thirty minutes later, Cassia was yet again in the back of another deputy car, this time holding Jane's hand. Deputy Chester had promised to meet them at the station and bring some board and video games. He was even going to bring in a small TV.

The landscape whizzed by, making Cassia feel even more dizzy than she already felt from exhaustion. She'd only had a few hours' sleep the previous night and now was really feeling it. A stomach full of sugary pancakes had helped a bit, but now the sugar was wearing off.

Cassia checked her phone. Only ten percent power left and a bunch of spam notifications. Looking closely, she realized she had missed a call. It was from the law firm in New York. A thrill of excitement hit her, until she realized it was the weekend, and things were a little busy right now any how to deal with something like that. But they had finally called her back. She felt like this must be good news, unless they were in the habit of calling to give bad news, which judging by the sarcastic tone of their answering guy, might be a possibility.

Jane looked at Cassia and Cassia bashfully put her phone back in her pocket and tried to make small talk with Jane all the way to the station.

Somewhere behind them, Genevieve was following in her blue Honda to give Cassia a ride home. Cassia was hoping they could settle Jane in at the station for a nap, at least, since the girl had also had no sleep all night, so Cassia could go home and take a nap as well. Once the girl's adrenaline wore off, she would surely crash. Even now, Cassia caught Jane's eyes drooping once in a while.

———

Genevieve and Cassia sat inside Genevieve's car with both doors open in the late afternoon sunlight in the parking lot of the K-Okay gas station just outside of town. The parking lot stood mostly empty, and the green and red stripes across the front of the building looked so old and faded that Cassia would have thought the place was closed if they hadn't just been in there getting slushy ice drinks loaded with sugar. "Need the sugar to make it home and I'm all out of car supplies," Genevieve said.

The day had warmed up, once again feeling like summer. It almost didn't feel right to have such a perfectly beautiful day when so many bad things were happening.

Genevieve and Cassia drank half their drinks, then placed the rest in the cup holder in the middle and leaned their seats back to take a small nap. A pleasant breeze blew through the open car doors, almost feeling like nature was lulling them to sleep.

One benefit of resting while still in town was they were close by in case there was an emergency with Jane. Deputy Chester had promised to call if the girl started to get upset. Hopefully that wouldn't happen anytime soon. The last Cassia had seen of Jane, she'd been settled down in the bunk in the sole prison cell, with a blanket thrown over her. Of course, the cell door had been open, but it still felt good to have both Deputy Chester and Sheriff Andrews there watching the girl. Sheriff Andrews had muttered something about having enough staff in case other departments visited. Cassia was starting to wonder if there was a soft gooey inside to his prickly exterior.

Picking up her drink, Cassia took a long pull through the straw until she felt her brain protest the sudden cold. The sugar made the drink almost irresistible, but she stopped drinking before she had a full-on headache, forcing herself to put it back down in the cup holder.

Genevieve already had her eyes closed and looked perfectly content laying back in the driver's seat.

Cassia leaned back into her own seat and closed her own eyes.

They sat in silence for a few moments. Nearby, birds chirped.

"So why did they call him Tricky Dick?" Cassia asked, still leaning back with her eyes closed.

"Hmmm?" Genevieve asked.

"The guy in the photo. Nixon."

"Oh, he was always getting himself into trouble. His problem is he recorded it. And then had to turn over the tapes."

"What did he do?" Cassia asked.

"Something to do with illegally doing stuff to his enemies. I don't remember those school lessons anymore," Genevieve said. "I just liked the name. Something like that would go viral now in no time. Faster even."

"Hmmm," Cassia said. She was starting to drift off. "How dumb to record yourself doing bad stuff."

Cassia fell into a light sleep, while the distant sounds of a car driving through town, or a child calling out, kept her from falling too deeply. Something was bothering her too, and she couldn't quite figure it out. Sort of like sleeping on a pea through ten mattresses; she could tell something was there but couldn't figure out what it was.

After tossing and turning in the car seat several times, and earning a one-eyed glare from Genevieve, Cassia decided to get up and walk a bit around the parking lot.

She stared at the old building. At one time it had been new and shiny, but now the paint was faded from the sun, and wires hung from the security camera, apparently no longer hooked up.

She stopped pacing. The security camera. She hurried back to the car and leaned in through the passenger window while hanging onto the doorframe.

"Genevieve," she said. "Gen!"

Genevieve slowly opened one eye. "What. You're impossible. All I want is twenty minutes—"

"Do they have security cameras at the Wild Horses Banquet Hall?"

Genevieve stared at her, her mouth still open from her unfinished sentence. Finally, she said, "I don't know."

"Would Roger know?" Cassia asked.

"Maybe? If anyone in this town did, it would be him, I'd guess."

Cassia didn't have to say anything else. Genevieve pulled the lever to bring her seat to an upright position, and then pulled out her phone and dialed Roger.

Cassia climbed into the passenger seat and waited.

They didn't have to wait long. Cassia could hear a faint hello on the other end.

"Roger, my man. You wouldn't happen to do any work at the Wild Horses Banquet Hall, would you?" Genevieve asked.

Grasping her hands nervously, Cassia wished Genevieve would put the phone on speaker, but didn't want to interrupt her to say so. Instead, she leaned in, trying to hear something, but it was no use. Only a faint rumble came through to her.

"No way," Genevieve said. Cassia gave her a look, wanting to know what was going on, but Genevieve just held up one finger for Cassia to wait. "That is a sort of a coincidence. When did you get the call? No wait, don't tell me. I'm dying for some of your cookies, so I'll just stop by and say hi in person."

Genevieve hung up the phone. She pursed her lips before sliding the phone into the middle console and starting the car.

Cassia couldn't stand it anymore. "Well?" she asked. "Why did you get off the phone so fast?"

Giving her a grim look, Genevieve only said, "Plausible deniability."

CHAPTER 21

Cassia, Genevieve, and Roger sat on Roger's front stoop munching cookies. Tiny little lights in the bushes that Cassia had never noticed before blinked in the late afternoon sun.

Roger wore blue mechanic overalls and had grease on his nose. He had been working on his latest creation in the backyard and hadn't had time to change before they came over.

"So they called you to do some repair work on a camera system?" Genevieve asked, wiping crumbs off her lap.

"Yeah, but it was weird looking. It didn't look like natural damage. More like someone had grabbed the wires and yanked. Recently. The wall hadn't even gotten dirty behind where the wires were hanging down."

"So they did have a camera system? Or they do have?" Cassia asked.

"Yes. One of those fancy ones too." Roger said. His eyes lit up, like they always did when he was talking about complicated machinery.

"What do you mean, fancy?" Genevieve asked.

"Like it transmits off-site. Most of them write to tapes too, but the really nice ones also send the data somewhere else in case anything happens to the main system," Roger said. He tried to wipe his hands off on his overalls, but didn't get his hands any cleaner and only got new cookie grease on the knee of his overalls.

"To some data storage thing?" Cassia asked. She was thinking of some telescopes that would send the data to multiple data centers around the world, allowing for people to pull it remotely even if they weren't on-site. But who wouldn't want to be on-site when the site was some exotic location like a high mountain top, or beautiful desert scene? She shook her head, forcing herself back to the current situation.

"Or stream to someone's computer," Roger said.

"Can someone watch those camera systems live?" Genevieve asked.

"Of course," Roger said. "Well… with many streaming systems you can."

"I mean, like watching live at some faraway location," Genevieve said to clarify.

"I don't see why not."

They sat in silence for a moment. Genevieve picked apart a piece of grass she had plucked from the lawn while she thought. "Did you see anything else unusual there?"

"Not really, but I wasn't really looking, either. There is some construction in the back. I only know that because it was noisy and making the floors shake," Roger said

Cassi could not remember any construction going on behind the Wild Horses Banquet Hall. The building seemed old, and not getting much new attention.

Roger shifted uncomfortably in his seat and gave a little cough. "Do you guys want anything to drink?"

"I do," Cassia said.

Roger got up and went inside the house, the screen door slamming behind him.

Genevieve looked over at Cassia. "Sheriff Andrews or Deputy Waters say anything to you about videotape?"

"No. What about your interrogators?" Cassia asked.

"Not a word. That seems sort of strange."

"Maybe the cameras weren't working, and now that there was a problem, they want to fix them," Cassia said.

Genevieve threw away her discarded bits of greenery and reached over the lawn to get a fresh piece of grass. "Too bad it would be too late to help us if the system really was broken then."

They sat in silence for a few moments, listening to the sounds of Roger inside the house filling glasses with ice and pouring something into them.

"If the cameras *were* working the night of Polina's death..." Cassia said. "I wonder what they would show? Jane seems awfully convinced that her father wouldn't do anything to hurt anyone."

"That could just be loyalty," Genevieve said. "Or denial."

"Could be." Much as Cassia hated it, she had to agree. Who thought their parents were really monsters? Some people, obviously, but Jane wasn't one of them.

The screen door opened again and Roger came out balancing three glasses of lemonade. Cassia eagerly reached up for a glass. She remembered how good it was before.

Genevieve took her own glass, took a long sip, and then nodded thanks to him. After a satisfied sigh, she asked, "Roger, would it be possible to head down to the Wild Horses and maybe take a look for some tapes to that system?"

"Maybe," Roger said as he sat down. "Luckily for that, I haven't finished all the work yet, although Deputy Waters did insist on getting the key back until the parts came in for me to complete it."

"Deputy Waters?" Cassia asked.

"Yeah, he owns the place," Roger said.

A stunned silence overcame Cassia and Genevieve. Roger drank more of his lemonade, not noticing it at first.

"What you mean, Deputy Waters owns Wild Horses? The whole thing?" Genevieve asked.

"That I don't know," Roger said. "At least part of it. He was the one who gave me the keys. Most places like that are owned by a group, or at least that's what I've seen in my jobs..."

Cassia leaned forward, her elbows on her knees, trying to remember how Deputy Waters had acted when he showed up at the hall that night. It seemed like he had just acted like any other law enforcement person. Well, maybe bossier than most, but that didn't mean much. Plus, someone else had unlocked the place for the movie people, but Cassia couldn't remember Deputy Waters even going over and talking to them.

Not that she'd been able to see everything that happened that night, or even been thinking clearly, after seeing Polina's body in the grass.

"Ugh, we need more information," Genevieve said.

"You guys sure the ex-husband didn't do it?" Roger asked. "Seems like it's always the ex in the papers and stuff when there is a murder story."

Cassia and Genevieve exchanged glances. "Yes," they said in unison.

"Yes?" Roger asked, confused.

"Yes, I don't think he did it. It seems too pat," Genevieve said.

"And his daughter doesn't think he could do it," Cassia added. "Besides, it looked like he had just shown up to the place when I found the body. There were people crawling all over there. So how could Ricardo have done anything?"

"Well someone did something," Roger said.

"True," Cassia said. An image of Polina's awful position in the grass flashed back to her, a brutal reminder of that night.

It was a memory she really didn't want to have.

"We really need to know if those cameras were working that day," Genevieve said.

———

Cassia and Genevieve stood outside Genevieve's car in front of the Mandress mansion. Cassia talked on the phone and paced agitatedly while Genevieve watched. Around them the dark was settling in, giving the place a slightly ominous feel.

Miss Mansfield meowed from inside the place, loud enough to be heard through the front door. The cat was not happy with their delay in coming in when they'd arrived home.

"What do you mean, she freaked out?" Cassia asked, freaking out a little herself. They had called Deputy Chester about half an hour before when deciding if it was safe to make the long drive back to the mansion or not. He'd said everything was fine. The child protective services lady had come, and apparently charmed Jane enough for the girl to be okay going with her.

It seemed everything was going to be okay, at least for a day or two.

And Cassia really needed a day or two of okay. She had not had a good night's sleep in the last forty-eight hours and it was hitting her hard.

Fuzzy brain, not-thinking-well hard.

They had just pulled up to the mansion when Cassia's phone had rung, with an unusually excited and upset Deputy Chester on the other end.

The call was not good news, to put it mildly.

Afterwards, Cassia got off the phone, feeling even more off-kilter than she had before.

"What was that all about?" Genevieve asked.

"Apparently Deputy Waters showed up with Lucas before Jane and social services could leave. Jane had a screaming fit, and then tried to hide behind Deputy Chester. He sounded a little traumatized by the whole thing."

"She got that riled up again?" Genevieve asked.

"Yeah. And after we worked so hard to calm her down," Cassia said.

"Something weird is up with that girl," Genevieve said. "She wasn't like that when we saw her at the dance studio."

"No," Cassia said, agreeing. "Shy, yes. Freaking out, no."

"Well, except for when Polina showed up. Then she seemed to be a little freaking out."

"But not screaming," Cassia said.

"No. We have to figure out what's happening. We can't leave her in this horrible situation. Our recon can't come soon enough." The resolve on Genevieve's face matched the determination Cassia felt.

———

Eight hours and some much-needed sleep later, Cassia found herself on a hill overlooking the Wild Horses Banquet Hall. Overhead a partial moon shed light on the building and surrounding greenery. The police tape still lined the back; there was also a lift bucket there, its orange base and claw looking like a monstrous angular animal crouched next to the building.

Next to her, Genevieve crouched, a black knit hat pulled over her blue hair. She wore all black and had even put black smudges on her face. Genevieve always got completely into the role, no matter what it was.

On Cassia's other side, Roger crouched. His fluffy white hair also been pushed into a black knit hat and his coveralls exchanged for tightfitting black clothing. He'd walked awkwardly in the clothing Genevieve had given him out of the vast resources that was her backseat. Tight fitting was not his thing.

Cassia didn't even want to know how Genevieve had clothing Roger's size, or almost his size.

Of course Cassia had on all black as well. Genevieve had insisted.

Despite their best efforts, Cassia couldn't help but think they probably looked more like those ridiculous pictures of the three wise monkeys than serious burglars.

"You sure this is better than just asking for the keys so Roger can walk in the front?" Cassia asked.

"He'd have to ask Deputy Waters for the key, otherwise it would look weird, considering that Waters was the one who hired him," Genevieve said. "The last thing we want is Deputy Waters thinking about some stranger being here."

"True that," Cassia said, her heart sinking a little. The last time they snuck into a place, they'd ended up getting shot at and nearly poisoned with carbon monoxide.

Hopefully this time would be nothing like that.

Her stomach twisted in anxiety, apparently not believing in hope.

They'd parked off a back side road, tucking Roger's old truck into a grouping of pine trees, hiding it from the rarely traveled road. The truck was old enough that it could easily look like it had been abandoned there, and even if someone recognized it as Roger's truck, that was a common enough sight in the region. Most people knew Roger, or someone who used Roger as a handyman. Hopefully it was as unremarkable as the sun in the sky.

Genevieve stood, picking up the circular loop of rope they'd brought and hoisting it on her shoulder. "Ready?" She checked her phone. "It's 4 am exactly. We should have at least two hours before anyone is due for work. Let's do this thing."

Cassia and Roger stood.

"You sure there's not an alarm system?" Cassia asked Roger, just wanting to make sure one more time before they went and did something stupid.

"I'm sure," Roger said.

"Well, that's it," Genevieve said. "Let's find some tapes."

The three took off down the hill to go break into the Wild Horses Banquet Hall.

CHAPTER 22

Cassia, Genevieve, and Roger walked and sometimes slipped down the hill to the Wild Horses Banquet Hall. The partial moon helped illuminate the way, but it was still difficult to see, especially with the masses of dead leaves and debris littering the ground, leaving the hillside unkempt and wild. Only the grass closer to the low sprawling building was mowed and tended to.

Unfortunately, the grass was all that grew close to the building. There was little in the way of landscaping around the place, so once they left the relative shelter of the trees and underbrush of the hill they would be completely exposed.

In their favor, dawn was safely some time away. No pink yet tinged the eastern sky.

Reaching the edge of the tree line, they stopped.

Genevieve pointed to the back of the building where the monstrous bucket truck stood. "Let's start there. We never got a good look at anything since they hustled us away from the body so quickly."

The back area looked much as Cassia remembered it, except the grass was trampled completely flat, no longer high around the corner where the gardener had been sloppy and not mowed well. She could almost see where Polina's body had lain. That spot was almost directly under the bucket of the bucket truck, something she thought weird until she looked up.

A piece of wrought iron railing hung precariously by two bolts on one side from a third-floor balcony.

Roger and Genevieve walked to Cassia and joined her, staring up at the balcony.

"I guess we know what happened to Polina," Cassia said.

"That would probably do it," Genevieve said. Looking down from the balcony, Genevieve walked around the ground, tapping it with her feet. "Though it is all grass and dirt out here. Would you necessarily break your neck if you didn't fall onto concrete?"

Cassia shrugged. She had no idea.

Roger scanned the building, then pointed excitedly to the high far corner on the back of the building.

"Bingo," he said.

A security camera pointed down and into the middle of the back of the building, aiming directly at the door at the back.

"Are the wires attached to that one?" Genevieve asked.

Roger squinted at it. "I can't see."

Cassia pulled out her phone and took a zoomed-in picture of the security camera. Enlarging the image on her phone, she squinted at it, but it was too blurry and pixilated to tell if the camera was in good shape or not. It was just too dark out.

"Let me try," Genevieve said, pulling out her newer phone. She zoomed in on the camera and took a photo with a surprisingly bright flash. Her photo clearly showed the dangling wires hanging from the back of the camera, not attached to anything.

"Thank goodness," Cassia said, finally relieved enough to voice her first thought. "If that camera had been working, we would've all been busted."

"If that camera had been working, we'd know exactly what happened to Polina," Genevieve pointed out.

"If it actually happened out here," Roger said. He checked the camera angle against the position of the balcony.

"True that," Cassia said, agreeing.

They stood in silence for a moment, staring at the spot that had been Polina's last outside time on the grass while not in a casket.

Roger sighed. "Unless they hired someone else to fix it, the system shouldn't be working at all. I left it off because I'm still waiting for parts."

Genevieve clapped Roger on the back. "Never thought I'd be happy for something like that."

———

Roger pulled out a small case from his pants pocket and approached the back door. Curious, Cassia followed. She'd never seen anyone pick a lock before, except in movies, and who knew how accurate that was. Probably not at all.

Taking out a few items from the case, he zipped it back up and put it back in his pocket, then stepped up to the lock. He inserted a flat piece of metal in the bottom of the lock, holding it with his left hand, while reaching in with a tiny little metal hook with his right. His face took on a look of intense concentration as he wiggled the hook with his right hand in a seemingly random set of motions.

Cassia opened her mouth to ask a question, but before she could Genevieve bumped her shoulder to get her attention and then shook her head at Cassia.

Right, no distracting someone while they're working.

Sooner than Cassia expected, the lock gave a soft click and Roger used the flat piece of metal to turn the lock completely. He pulled the door open, and only then released the flat piece of metal to let the lock slide back into place. He beamed at their silent claps.

They filed into the dark space. Metal and tile gleamed around them. They'd entered through the kitchen. Not a place of happy memories for Cassia, but at least it was uncluttered and easy to see if there was no one in there.

Luckily for them, none of the interior doors were locked inside the building. The owners must be so confident of the exterior security that they didn't even bother. It helped that there was only one business inside—the banquet hall.

———

The flat low carpet and neutral walls were even more depressing at night when the place was empty of people. They each had a small flashlight, sending them over the walls and doors instead of turning on the main lights. The beams of light were probably still visible from the outside, but not nearly so much as if they had set everything blazing with the overhead fluorescents.

"Where was the broken camera?" Cassia asked.

Roger pointed upstairs. They followed him to the main open staircase at the front of the building, climbing quickly up to the second floor, then down the hall to the enclosed staircase that led up to the more private third floor. The third floor was only half of the building, comprised of a long narrow hallway with doors set in it and an open space in the back that looked like an employee break room. Off the break room stood the balcony with the broken wrought iron railing. It was visible through the glass doors that led out to the concrete platform.

The camera Roger was talking about was at the far end of the hall from the break area. It pointed down the hall and directly at the balcony.

"Well, shin and shinola. That would be exactly the camera we'd need to see what happened if Polina fell," Genevieve said.

Cassia had to agree. It was beyond weird that camera would be the one that Roger was called in to fix. What about the camera outside that also appeared broken? How convenient for both of them to not work.

"The rest of the system is downstairs," Roger said, after they had taken a moment to go down the hallway to the break area and examine the door to the balcony. Roger could have picked the lock, but considering the bad state of the railing, and the stains on the balcony itself, Cassia wasn't sure she'd be willing to step foot on the thing. It did not look stable.

"Downstairs it is," Genevieve said. Somehow, Genevieve had taken the position as captain of their little group. Cassia didn't mind. Besides, Genevieve knew Roger much better than she did.

He led them downstairs by the enclosed stairwell, which went down one floor past the main floor, into a dim basement of sorts. There were no windows here, so Roger flicked on the lights, sending bright light bouncing off painted white cinderblocks. It felt almost physically painful to Cassia, and she squeezed her eyes shut, feeling them water.

"Little warning next time," Cassia said.

"Right. Sorry," Roger said, his own eyes screwed shut. It made Cassia feel only the tiniest bit better that he was suffering from the mistake too.

After what felt like a long time, Cassia could finally bear to squint down the hall. There were only two doorways—a normal size door that looked like it led to an office and a set of double metal doors at the far end. Roger pointed to the double set of doors.

But when they got there, he groaned.

A thick metal chain wrapped around the doors, and was clasped shut with a combination lock.

"That is new," he said, pointing to the lock. "I'm not prepared for that." He looked glum.

Genevieve, however, was grinning, and rubbed her hands excitedly. "Have no fear. I can do this one."

Pushing between Cassia and Roger to reach the lock, Genevieve gave it a good tug and spun the dial. Then she held the lock in her left hand with her fingers around the shank and spun it with the right. "Write down these numbers," she said over her shoulder.

Cassia grabbed her phone out of her pocket and pulled up her notes function. Genevieve called out eight numbers after a lot of spinning and yanking on the lock.

Frowning as the numbers kept coming, Cassia finally said, "That's too many. Don't you only need three?"

Genevieve ignored her as she fiddled with the lock a bit longer, and then finally set it down. "That's it. Okay, let me see the numbers."

Cassia held up her phone to Genevieve, who glanced through the numbers and picked three of them.

Turning back around, Genevieve spun the lock several times, then dialed the numbers in and gave the lock a swift yank.

It opened with a pop.

"No way," Cassia said, impressed and a bit shocked at the same time. Who were these people, and how did they know how to break into everything?

Genevieve unwound the chain and pulled open the doors. The inside of this room had a bare concrete floor and wasn't finished like the hallway with linoleum tile. Uncovered pipes ran the length of the room, and an enormous electrical panel and an equally monstrous boiler took spots along the wall. Further down from both of those, a small desk sat with some monitors on top of it, along with an opened black equipment box with scattered tools around it.

Roger walked to the desk and pointed at the black box. "The main system." Hidden behind the main box, another small metal box sat, along with some network equipment.

On the desk behind the system boxes, stacks of tiny mini tapes lined up against the wall. The partially disassembled box itself had a space for two tapes, of which both were full.

"That looks really old," Genevieve said, not impressed.

Roger shrugged. "As long as it works, I guess. It's not that bad. It did have the add-on for off-site data." He pointed to the second black box and a router sitting on top of it. Green lights flashed on the router. At least that was working.

If that was a good thing.

Pulling out one of the tapes from the black box, Roger held it up. "I didn't think to bring a player. Not that I think I have a player small enough to lug around."

Genevieve and Cassia frowned at the pile of tapes and their new problem.

"You think they'd miss them if we took a few? Or all of them?" Genevieve asked.

"I don't know—," Roger said, stopping as they all three heard banging vibrating in the building and distant voices.

"Someone's here," Genevieve said, while Cassia said, "No no no no." They actually both ran around for a few seconds like panicked chickens before Genevieve grabbed Cassia by the upper arms and said, "Calm yourself, girl."

Cassia nodded. Genevieve took her own advice as well.

Meanwhile, Roger had slipped the tape in his hand into his shirt pocket and ran back to the door and grabbed the lock and chain. He flicked the light off on the way back, getting Cassia and Genevieve's attention as they were suddenly plunged into darkness.

"There's no place to hide in here. Come on," Roger said, his voice floating through the dark to them before he opened the door to the hall, letting the light into the room.

All three piled out the door and Roger wrapped the chain and set the lock by giving it a good spin. They ran down the hall to the smaller door, which luckily opened. Inside, it looked like it was supposed to be an office with several large cubicles, but instead it was stuffed full of boxes with images of plates, glassware, and paper products on the outside.

"Huzzah for too much stock," Genevieve muttered as they ran around the stacks of boxes and nestled behind them, pushing up to the wall behind as much as they could to stay out of eyesight of anyone at the door. There was just enough space for the three of them, all except for a bit of Roger's feet, which poked out to one side no matter how much he twisted his long limbs. Hopefully they would just look like strange shaped black shadows.

"I thought this was way too early for people to come in," Cassia asked, a crack of panic in her voice.

"Shhhh," Genevieve hissed at her.

A moment later, the door from the stairwell banged open, and a voice boomed in the hallway. "What the heck are the lights doing on?"

CHAPTER 23

Cassia shivered as the door banged open in the hallway outside the small office turned supply room that Cassia, Genevieve, and Roger huddled in, trying to hide in the darkness and chaos in the room. The smell of dust tickled Cassia's nose. The dust must have been thrown into the air when the three of them rushed in to hide behind the cardboard boxes stacked in the room.

Cassia put her hands on the box in front of her. It felt full and stiff, but still not nearly enough protection against whatever was out there. They sounded angry.

She leaned to the left to peek out at floor level around the boxes. The only light in the room came from the thin gap under the door to the hall outside. None of them had turned on the lights when they'd rushed in, instead counting on the light spilling from the hallway when they ran in to find their hiding spots.

"Do you think I'm made of money?" the irate voice in the hall asked again. It sounded familiar. The shadows of two sets of feet passed by the office door and went on to the double doors at the end of the hall into the machine room. Whoever was with the angry person didn't speak loud enough to be heard inside the office.

The clinking of the chains on the door in the hallway filtered into the room they sat in, mixing with the sounds of Cassia, Genevieve, and Roger breathing heavily. Cassia had tried to hold her breath at first, but quickly grew dizzy and realized that was not going to work. It was easier to breathe now that whoever was out there was focused on the other door.

It only took a moment for the chain to fall free and the other door to open and slam shut again behind the two people. Cassia glanced back at Roger and Genevieve. She couldn't see more than dark shadows in the room. It unnerved her to not be able to see their faces.

Genevieve pulled out her small flashlight, aimed it at the cardboard box next to her, let the light bounce back and fill their tiny spot. Cassia winced at the clicking noise of the flashlight switch, though rationally she knew the two people out there couldn't hear it. Genevieve held up two fingers, her eyebrows raised in question. Cassia nodded. Genevieve flicked the light off again.

They waited in darkness.

When nothing happened after a few minutes, Genevieve pulled at Cassia's sleeve, yanking her back toward her and Roger. Once Cassia was closer, Genevieve leaned in and whispered, "Maybe we should try to leave. Run for it while they are in that room. They could be in there for hours, and we will really be trapped when everyone else shows up for work."

Genevieve had a good point, but the thought of leaving the room while knowing there were two people out there terrified Cassia. Being scared did not help her ability to calculate odds.

At all.

"I agree," Roger said quietly. "Let's—"

Before he could finish his sentence, the door to the machine room slammed open. It seemed to be the de facto mannerism for whoever was out there. Slam, slam, slam.

The clinking of the chains followed. They must be putting the lock back on again.

"Find the one I told you about, and wipe the rest," Angry Voice said.

"All of them? Don't you think we need—" a meeker male voice said.

"Just do as I say, got it?" Angry Voice said.

There was no response from the other person.

Just then Genevieve dropped her flashlight, and it fell with a hollow clink on the linoleum clad concrete floor. A wave of fear washed over Cassia, just as a voice outside exclaimed, "What was that?"

It was nothing, nothing, Cassia thought, as if she could force that notion into the head of the person outside.

"Is someone in here?" Angry Voice asked. "No one is supposed to be in here without prior authorization."

"I'm sure it was nothing," the second person said. "Maybe a mouse."

"A mouse? This is a banquet hall. We can't be having mice. Do I have to do everything myself?"

Without warning, the door to the office space flew open and slammed into a stack of boxes parked too close to it.

"Why is this packed full of stuff?" Angry Voice sounded even angrier. And intensely, terrifyingly, close. In the room they were in, even.

Cassia concentrated on not peeing her pants.

Light from the hallway filtered over and she glanced back at Roger and Genevieve. Roger was in an awkward position with his legs behind Cassia, but both he and Genevieve had their little flashlights out, ready to strike back, as if that would do anything to the person who was more than likely standing above them.

The situation was ludicrous. Besides being terrified, Cassia had the almost overwhelming urge to laugh like a maniac. She held her hands over her mouth and pressed hard.

Angry Voice took one step into the room, and then a radio with the volume turned up painfully high crackled to life at his hip. "Deputy Waters," a voice called over the radio, the signal coming in and out, struggling with the concrete basement.

"Dammit," Angry Voice said. "I gotta go." He stepped back into the hallway and the door gently swung shut. In the hallway, he said to the other person, "Just do what I say and let me know when you're done."

Angry Voice clomped to the stairwell door and exited.

Cassia, Genevieve, and Roger held their breath, waiting.

A few moments later, after what might have been some muttered venting outside, a second set of footsteps followed, leaving the basement quiet.

Holy cow, Angry Voice was Deputy Waters.

———

They sat in silence for a few minutes, waiting to make sure no one else was in the basement outside that door. Finally, Genevieve pulled out her phone and checked the time. "It's almost six. We have to get out of here. Let's grab what we can and go."

They picked themselves up off the floor and felt their way to the door. The light in the hallway was now off, robbing the room of what little light it did have before.

Once they were out in the hallway, Cassia flipped on the flashlight on her phone, regretting not doing it sooner. She didn't dare turn on the hallway lights in case they had to run and hide again.

Hopefully not. Cassia's heart couldn't take it.

"Do you still have that list of numbers?" Genevieve asked.

Cassia pulled them up on her phone and showed them to Genevieve. It was much quicker getting in the room the second time.

They rushed to the table with the camera system, but the stack of many tapes that had been lined up at the back of the desk were gone.

Every single one of them.

"No no no," Cassia said. They came all this way for nothing.

"I knew we should grab them and run," Genevieve said, rubbing her head in frustration.

"We do have one," Roger said, pulling the lone tape from his shirt pocket.

————

It was an agonizingly slow trip to get out of the basement and out the door of the Wild Horses Banquet Hall. They crept along at every stretch, listening so hard Cassia almost thought that she could feel her ears tingling, but no strange noises reached them. No people walking or talking. No banging doors. Just the sound of the HVAC system turning on.

They finally made their way to the kitchen and cracked open the back door. A beautiful pink glowed in the east, promising a sunrise coming soon. The landscape was quiet and still, the stubbly cornfield in the back looking a lot less ominous now that it was light out.

Not a car sat in the back field, or anywhere they could see from the door. They cautiously exited the building.

Creeping along the side of the building, Cassia checked around the corner. No cars there either, nor around the front. Whoever had been inside along with them was long gone.

Cassia and Roger headed for the tree line. It took a few minutes for Cassia to realize that Genevieve wasn't with them.

Panicked, she turned around and saw her running to catch up, looking like a human embodiment of a shadow in her all black outfit and dark smudges across her face.

"Sorry. Wanted to get a picture of that picker unit. Never knowing when that information might come in handy," Genevieve said as she reached them.

They climbed the hill and reached Roger's truck, sitting just as they left it, except now with the faint sheen of dew on it. Cassia grimaced and looked down at her feet. The only other tennis shoes she'd been able to find in her boxes had been her thin black shoes that were supposed to be like running barefoot. Now they just felt like walking in the wet grass barefoot. Was she ever going to have dry feet for longer than a few hours?

They drove in silence straight to Roger's house, and then filed into his basement to sit at stools in front of his massive workbench that now held an antique mini tape system he'd been using to teach himself about the one at the Wild Horses.

Cassia couldn't help but look around at all the other equipment jam-packed in the tiny space, crammed into large industrial shelving units and piled everywhere along the walls. Really, the space wasn't that small, it was just completely filled with stuff. There were wood and cardboard boxes labeled 'velvet', and 'wrenches', and 'screws, sizes 1 to 9', along with plastic bins, some clear-sided, showing everything from teapots to broken bits of machinery with wires hanging off and transistors showing, the pieces so far removed from their purpose that she couldn't even guess what they actually were for. There was even what looked like a full-sized industrial drill press right out of shop class. Who has something like that in their home?

Roger looked completely comfortable in this chaos. He was surrounded by his favorite things.

Impatient, Genevieve had no attention for their surroundings. She motioned for Roger to hurry as he took the tape from his pocket and put it in the ancient machine. He pressed down on the mechanism and turned the monitor on. An old CRT monitor hummed as it warmed up. It looked weird to see such an old screen, even for this setup.

They were in luck, sort of. After about five minutes of black-and-white static, the image crawled down from the top of the screen and slowly came into focus. It was the third-floor hallway. The camera that was supposedly broken. It hadn't been broken for this tape, instead showing a clear view down the third-floor hallway toward the balcony.

"Bless the goddess," Genevieve said.

Cassia was too tired and too happy at their luck to even react to yet another strange saying that Genevieve had.

Roger was apparently used to them.

But after twenty minutes of watching the static picture, Cassia's hopes began to droop.

"How long can these tapes go on for?" Genevieve asked.

"The expensive ones… six hours, I think," Roger said.

Cassia groaned.

"We don't have to sit here for six hours though," Roger said. "The system isn't that old."

He pressed the fast-forward button, and they watched sped up images of the hallway. The image itself slowly drifted up the monitor in a hypnotic pattern. Despite herself, Cassia felt her eyes drooping. She pinched herself to wake herself up. It barely worked.

Then a shadow raced across the screen.

"Wait, go back," Genevieve said, noticing it at the same time.

Roger rewound the tape and then started it up again at regular speed.

The shadowy figure was Polina. She walked from the stairwell back toward the balcony in high-heeled shoes and an expensive looking beige skirt set that looked ill-suited for a night of directing a movie outside.

Was that what Polina had been wearing when she found her? Cassia couldn't remember. All she could remember was the horrible angle of the woman's neck.

On screen, Polina made herself a cup of coffee at the machine on the counter in the back. A few moments later, Jane walked down the hallway toward Polina, slowly, as if going to her own funeral. Ricardo was behind her.

"Jane?" Cassia said, surprised.

"And Ricardo," Genevieve said, grimly.

Just then, the tape player made a horrible squeal and locked up. Roger leapt up from his chair and turned it off, but he was too slow. When he opened the door to the tape compartment, a pile of loose tape popped out.

CHAPTER 24

Nothing in the basement moved as Cassia, Genevieve, and Roger stared down at the pile of tape in his hands. It almost felt as if everything in the dusty basement held its breath for a moment.

Emotions washed over Cassia. Shock, then disbelief, and maybe a little fear.

Mostly shock.

Jane and Ricardo. Could he really be guilty?

"No worries," Roger said. "I can fix this. I can fix the tape, and I can fix the machine. It will just take me a little while."

"Good," Cassia said, grabbing onto the lifeline he was throwing. She made a decision. "Good, you do that and then call us." Cassia pulled her phone out of her pocket and checked the time. It was ten thirty in the morning.

Genevieve looked at her questioningly.

"I have an idea. I need a miracle for it," Cassia said. It was all she was willing to share for the moment. She dialed her phone and walked up the stairs as it rang.

And a miracle she got.

"Cassia," Nate's warm voice said at the other end. "I was going to call you in a bit. How did it go at the bank?"

The bank. Cassia had forgotten all about that not fun adventure.

"Uh, I'll tell you about that later. I have something a bit more urgent I need your help with. I thought you were in jury duty and I'd get your voicemail," Cassia said. She made it to Roger's front door and walked outside.

He laughed on the other end of the line. "I know I'm a lawyer, and I'm not supposed to say this, but I got lucky. Dismissed after a week. No case for me. No one likes the look of a big tall guy on their jury. Maybe it scares the defendants."

As it should, thought Cassia. He was big enough to squash most people with one hand, not that he would do any such thing.

"Are you free this morning?" Cassia asked.

"I am. I'm in the office, and nothing's planned because I thought I'd still be gone."

"Great. I'll be there in a few minutes." Cassia turned off her phone and looked back at Roger's house. Time to retrieve Genevieve for a ride.

———

Mrs. Anderson offered both Cassia and Genevieve coffee when they arrived at the law office. Mrs. Anderson stared at Genevieve's blue manga hair curiously, now free from the black knit cap she'd been wearing. It was hard to believe the two had never met before in such a tiny town.

They sat under the gold lettered windows in the law office waiting room. Genevieve had the same awed expression she'd had at the bank. Mrs. Anderson's beehive hairstyle got extra attention. Cassia was glad Nate had them waiting just so Genevieve could see Mrs. Anderson and her full-on avocado green typewriter in action. This was not something people would believe by words alone. Or at least she wouldn't have before coming to this town.

It was so quiet, Cassia wondered if they had soundproofed the place. Only the click click click of the typewriter keys echoed.

Thankfully, Nate came bounding out of his back office. "Sorry, sorry. Got a call from the missus I had to take."

Cassia nodded and stood along with Genevieve. Was she a bad person for wondering what Nate's wife looked like? Was she also abnormally tall? Or tiny and short, like all the clichés.

"Hello, Genevieve. Good to see you too. Do you both have off from the diner today?" Nate asked.

"Yeah, about that," Cassia said. "Have you not seen the news lately? The diner was closed this weekend, and Trent's got someone else covering for us today."

"News?" Nate asked as he led them into his office and motioned for them to sit down.

Cassia filled him in about what happened at the movie shoot, and with Jane. She didn't know exactly how to explain the tape situation, but she did manage to suggest there might be proof it wasn't a murder.

"I don't know, the motivation seems clear," Nate said.

Cassia bit her lip. Something was off here, but she couldn't quite figure it out. She needed to talk it out or something.

"There's something else, isn't there?" Nate asked.

"There is, but I can't quite figure out what," Cassia said.

"Yeah," Genevieve said, chiming in. "It just seems too neatly tied up with a bow."

Nate considered her words for a moment. "In situations like those, the best thing to do is to gather all the facts. What facts do you have, and which ones are new ones that you didn't have before, and others might not have had either?" he asked.

"One new fact—the biggest one for me—is that Deputy

Waters is part owner of the place where Polina died, but he didn't say anything about that to anybody. It didn't even seem like Sheriff Andrews knew it," Cassia said. "Could that be important?"

Nate's eyebrows rose. "Could that be important? Oh yes. Let me get some more information from you," he said as he pulled out a pen from the holder on his desk and grabbed a sheet of paper.

———

Genevieve drove the blue Honda through the winding roads to the Mandress mansion, the early morning sun having turned to late afternoon cloudiness. It matched Cassia's mood. She swore she could almost smell winter coming through the cracked window of the Honda that Genevieve insisted on having open to help keep her awake.

Glancing at Cassia, Genevieve asked, "Any word from Roger?"

Cassia checked her phone. "Last message says tape fixed, and he thinks the machine is close, but he's checking it on a different tape to keep the damage down."

"He's good. I'm sure he'll get it."

"I just hope he gets it soon," Cassia said. "I'm worried about Jane. That whole freak-out business is not cool."

"Yeah, me too."

"So how many brothers and sisters do you have, and where are they now?" Cassia asked.

"I have one younger brother, and that's enough. He ran away to Oregon or something. Not really run away," Genevieve said at Cassia's glance. "But he seems happier there than here."

"Do you ever miss him?" Cassia asked.

"Sometimes. But just sometimes, and if you ever meet him you're absolutely forbidden to tell him I said so."

"So that's why you're so good at chasing people down and tackling them," Cassia said. She tried to nudge the window shut without Genevieve noticing. Just a little less cold in the car would be nice, thank you very much.

"Is that what I did? I thought I was just showing someone how much we loved and cared about them," Genevieve said with a chuckle.

Cassia laughed, coming out more like a snort, which made her laugh even harder. Genevieve had to laugh at the snort as well.

"So..." Cassia said, trying to figure out the question. "If your younger brother was lying, what would you do to get him to tell the truth?"

Genevieve narrowed her eyes at Cassia before looking back at the road. "Let's just say this applies to more people than my brother, but the first step is always to find out what's important to them..."

The rest of the ride home was more of an education from Genevieve on how to deal with other people than Cassia ever thought she would get in one lifetime. She would have to remind herself on a regular basis to be very, very, careful around Genevieve in the future. That woman knew what she was doing.

———

Once again, Cassia had to make it up to Miss Mansfield, who was more than a little miffed at how much Cassia had been gone. After much fussing and cooing, Cassia could finally sit in her familiar perch at the island in the kitchen and stare at her phone, waiting for the two phone calls that would tell her what to do for Jane, if she could do anything at all.

First, the call came from Nate. He'd managed to pull amazing information during the last hours of the afternoon. Thank goodness for records moving online, and for real estate being mostly public records. Cassia could barely keep up writing her notes.

The second call was from Roger.

CHAPTER 25

Cassia and Genevieve waited outside the Bellard County sheriff's main station. It was situated off Highway 71, and not close to any specific town, so it felt especially cold and generic. Traffic whizzed by the white concrete station. Even the grass looked brown and dead.

Cassia clutched her coat tight. The unusually late summer had finally retreated to fall's awful advance. She hated her current lack of funds to buy a better winter coat. Being cold gets old.

"It's gonna be okay," Genevieve said, trying to reassure Cassia, misunderstanding her shivers.

Cassia nodded. She didn't bother clarifying. Truth was, she was nervous. This was her idea.

Moments later, Sheriff Andrews pulled up, Jane sitting in the front seat. Astoundingly, the girl was actually smiling. So was Sheriff Andrews until he glanced up and saw Cassia looking, and then his normal grumpy expression resumed its place on his face.

Great. Just like the cat. Was no one loyal to her?

Who was she kidding? She was lucky Sheriff Andrews wasn't trying to put her in jail every other day anymore.

Jane exited the car, practically bouncing.

"Excited to see your dad?" Cassia asked.

"Yes," Jane said.

"I'm sure he misses you, too. How did you do last night? How was…" Cassia didn't know the name of the woman Jane had stayed with. All she knew was they were approved by the state.

"Mrs. Ferris," Jane said, pronouncing the name carefully. "She made pancakes."

"More pancakes?" Genevieve asked, mock scandalized. "Who's got all the adults wrapped around her little finger?"

Jane was smart enough to know she wasn't supposed to actually answer that question, but she was embarrassed enough to turn red anyhow.

Like Genevieve should talk, Cassia thought cynically. Maybe Genevieve was taking notes from Jane on how to improve her manipulation skills.

Nah, not possible.

A second squad car pulled up on the far side of Sheriff Andrews' car. Deputy Chester put it in park and looked over at his passenger, Lucas Baros. Baros had been allowed to ride in the front seat, Cassia noted with a mixture of admittedly petty resentment and jealousy as the two men exited the car.

Jane turned around slowly to see what Cassia, Genevieve, and Sheriff Andrews were looking at. Her eyes locked on her grandfather and she froze. Everyone watched.

After only a moment's hesitation, Jane squealed and ran to hug her grandfather.

Cassia and Genevieve's eyes met.

"That's one question answered," Genevieve said.

———

Jane walked into the station between Cassia and her grandfather, Lucas. She was just a little too old to be willing to hold their hands, something Cassia regretted, but even she was not so ignorant of the way of kids as to embarrass the girl. Genevieve and Sheriff Andrews followed, leaving Deputy Chester by the cars.

The front entryway of the sheriff station was just as modern and angular and cold as the exterior was. Behind a large reinforced plastic barrier, two guards sat at a counter with tiny windows in front of them.

The leftmost officer, a blonde woman with a ponytail, leaned forward and spoke into a microphone for her window. "Can I help you?"

Sheriff Andrews stepped forward. "We're here to see Ricardo Baros."

The woman pointed to a clipboard on their side of the barrier with a pen on a chain attached. "Everyone sign in please and then send in one form of ID for each person." She pointed to the little drawer in front of the window.

Cassia could see Jane's mood deflating by the moment. They hadn't really warned her about where her dad was. They couldn't. Still, Cassia felt bad.

They got inside the inner waiting area, which felt more like a lobby, and waited on the wide orange cushioned chairs there. Someone would call them back. The inner lobby was also an essential corridor for the station. Deputies and workers walked through the various doors spread around the room leading to different destinations: offices, the break room, and the restrooms.

After a few moments of this, Jane started to relax, her breathing becoming more even.

Until Deputy Waters entered the room.

Cassia had never seen anyone literally crawl up on a chair and try to scoot away along the wall the way Jane did when she saw Deputy Waters. Sheriff Andrews grabbed the girl before she left the chair arrangement completely and set her down on the seat next to him. He didn't let go of her arm.

"Jane," Sheriff Andrews said very measuredly. "Do you know this man?"

Cassia just happened to glance up to see Deputy Waters give Jane a minute shake of his head. That jerk! He was trying to tell her what to say.

"Don't look at him," Cassia said to Jane quickly. "Just answer Sheriff Andrews' question."

"No," Jane said, her voice quivering.

Sheriff Andrews opened his mouth to speak, but hesitated, looking pained. Genevieve jumped in, coming to squat in front of the girl. "If you don't tell the truth here, your father and grandfather could be in a lot of trouble. A lot of trouble. It might be hard for you to see them again," Genevieve said.

"Hey!" Deputy Waters said, while Cassia protested at the same time, but for different reasons. Genevieve gave Cassia a warning look. Cassia leaned back in her seat.

Deputy Waters was not so easygoing.

"We don't hold with bullying children here," Deputy Waters said to Genevieve, conveniently ignoring the sheriff right next to her. "You can cut that out right now."

Sheriff Andrews bristled at the deputy's words, sending off enough angry energy that Cassia could feel it sitting next to him. If the deputy noticed, he didn't let on.

Genevieve asked again, not even bothering to look at Deputy Waters, who was now standing over. "Do you know this man?"

This time, Jane nodded. She looked terrified. Deputy Waters twitched, and for a horrifying moment Cassia thought he might actually have grabbed the girl if Genevieve hadn't been in the way.

"How do you know him?" Genevieve asked slowly, exuding a sense of calm.

Sheriff Andrews watched the exchange closely.

"He told me if I told anyone about my accident, everyone would go to jail, including me, and I would never see anyone ever again."

"Even after your father was taken away?" Genevieve asked. She looked pained to push on. Sheriff Andrews looked even more so, but he didn't stop the exchange.

Jane slowly nodded, tears starting down her face. "He said that would make it worse. He said my dad would hate me forever."

Cassia hissed.

Sheriff Andrews slowly moved his gaze up to Deputy Waters. "Now why would a young child say such a thing, do you think, Deputy Waters?"

The deputy took a step back, getting some distance from the sheriff's fierce glare. "Because she's a young kid who's making stuff up. I don't know her."

"And yet, she's terrified of you," Cassia said, her anger getting the better of her.

"It's her father she should be scared of. Isn't he the one killed his ex-wife? Her mother?" Deputy Waters said, pointing at Jane.

"Stepmother," Cassia muttered for Jane.

Sheriff Andrews stood. "That's enough. We have reason to believe the death of Polina Jan-Baros was an accident, and only made to look like a murder."

Deputy Waters backed up another step. He laughed, a little manically. "What kind of nutjob would make an accident look like a murder?"

Nate Perauski stepped forward. Cassia hadn't even noticed him come in with all that traffic in and out of the room. Roger stood next to him. Nate cleared his throat and spoke to Deputy

Waters. "One who doesn't have liability insurance anymore on his building and has been ignoring his staff's requests for basic maintenance for years. That could lead to a million little motivations… at least."

"Who is this?" Deputy Waters said, pointing at Nate, and starting to realize he was outnumbered.

"Just an interested lawyer," Nate said. He held up a sheaf of papers, but Cassia thought the fact that he was half a head taller than the deputy probably did more to intimidate the man.

"You have no proof it was an accident," Deputy Waters said.

"No, but Abra Data Services does," Roger said, leaning in closer to Deputy Waters and relishing to chance to clear things up for the man. Watching the video had not been easy. "I believe you are familiar with the video feed they run to your house? They keep copies on hard drives. With backups."

Deputy Waters gaped at that. His hands twitched. Roger stepped back.

"I must say, they respond very quickly to warrants," Sheriff Andrews said, smoothly stepping between Roger and Deputy Waters. He looked even more irate than usual. "Apparently they are not fans of making little girls lie just to save a few bucks."

Deputy Waters bolted.

Genevieve and Sheriff Andrews chased him down and grabbed him before he could get the door open.

CHAPTER 26

Deputy Chester and Jane sat cross-legged on the brown grass outside the Bellard County Sheriff's Station, each sipping their own juice box. Deputy Chester's looked like a toy with its tiny straw and little box nearly lost in his muscular hand. He wasn't as built like Sheriff Andrews, but he was larger than a kid's juice box sized person by about a dozen years.

Jane smiled and bobbed her head, the anxiety from earlier gone. Her only concern now was checking the door every few seconds.

The traffic still whizzed by, but somehow it didn't sound as stressful to Cassia as it had earlier. She sat next to Genevieve and watched the deputy and Jane. They'd turned down Deputy Chester's offer of juice from the vast offerings of his trunk to drink root beers from Genevieve's newly restocked backseat. The brown grass pricked through Cassia's pants, and the breeze blew a little chill, but she didn't care. Things were looking up.

There was just one more thing to take care of.

And Sheriff Andrews, Nate, and Roger were inside taking care of it.

Moments later, Jane's screams of happiness and her dashing to the door said their efforts had paid off. Ricardo and Lucas exited the station, blinking in the bright sun, followed by the rest of their crew. Jane ran into Ricardo's arms. He picked her up and swung her around like she was a kitten, an impressive feat of strength, since twelve-year-old girls are not small. Jane squealed and laughed.

Roger beamed at Cassia and Genevieve.

Even grumpy Sheriff Andrews had a ghost of a smile on his face. His muscles probably were not used to it.

Cassia and Genevieve got up, along with Deputy Chester, to join the group.

When Ricardo finally tired enough to set Jane down, Genevieve walked over and thumped him on the back. "Congrats. You're a free man."

"Thank you," Ricardo said in his ever charming Greek accent.

"What I don't understand," Genevieve said, "is why you didn't just tell them it had been an accident?"

Ricardo turned red and then glanced at Jane.

"Hey now," Sheriff Andrews said. "Let's not hassle the man."

Cassia whirled on Sheriff Andrews. Who was this person, and what had he done with the grump she was familiar with?

"No, no. It's okay," Ricardo said, holding a hand up to stop anyone else from giving Genevieve a hard time. "I knew I had done nothing, but until I could talk to a lawyer, I was not saying anything."

"Especially since you knew Jane had been in the back with Polina," Cassia said, guessing.

He nodded. She'd been right. Anything to protect his daughter.

Those two were definitely related.

Nate and Roger left immediately, citing work duties, but the rest of them had an impromptu picnic on the grass of the station of fruit leathers and stale crackers from Deputy Chester's trunk. They were waiting for just a few pieces of paperwork for Ricardo's release, and no one seemed to want to be the first to go. Cassia took the opportunity to sit next to Deputy Chester while Genevieve continued to drill Ricardo about business and social media. He must have the patience of a saint, because he only laughed and answered her in between answering his daughter's questions. That man definitely knew how to charm the ladies.

Cassia, for one, was glad to be out of his circle of influence for once. It was exhausting in there, fighting off all that charm. Deputy Chester was much more mellow.

"So, will you keep going to dance classes?" Cassia asked.

"Yes," Deputy Chester said. He took another bite of his fruit leather and chewed with the patience of a cow.

So much for conversation.

"Because of the redhead?" Cassia asked, feeling naughty.

Chester blushed, a remarkably cute thing on him. Cassia caught Sheriff Andrews staring at the two of them as if trying to figure out what was going on. She turned so he couldn't see her face. He huffed in annoyance.

"No. I mean, yes. I mean, both," Deputy Chester answered awkwardly.

Cassia eyed him. Something was bothering her. Maybe he'd be more forthcoming than Sheriff Andrews.

"Whatever happened to that Soren guy?" Cassia asked.

Deputy Chester blinked at the rapid change in subject.

"I mean, I thought we were suspected until you brought him in." Cassia said, still a little miffed to have been suspected of murdering someone. Again.

Deputy Chester laughed. "Everyone there was a suspect."

Cassia's mouth dropped open. Oh no, they didn't put her through all that worry for a general suspicion. Then it hit her.

They had.

She gritted her teeth, but managed to not say the retort that came to mind. Instead, she plastered on a smile. "So, what about Soren?"

Deputy Chester replied. "Yeah, I thought he was a goner. He said they got in a huge fight and all his damaged clothes were from falling down a hill after she made him get out of the car."

"Sounds like an unlikely story," Cassia said.

"Yup," Deputy Chester said.

Wow, even smarmy Soren was in her debt. It was a good day indeed.

CHAPTER 27

Nature graced them with one last beautiful warm Saturday before the oncoming winter hit. Cassia stood in the backyard of the mansion, messy as it was, and admired their decorating job of crepe paper ribbons and red and orange balloons. It was too late for any of the mansion's flowers, so the color had to come from somewhere.

From that, and the copper and silver sculpture Roger was setting up in the backyard. The first official Roger work on the Mandress property. It was a unique contribution that Cassia brought to the family estate, which made her irrationally proud. To make her even prouder, he was making her a smaller version of the rover Perseverance that he was making for the museum, but this one with air tube coming off it just like she had described in her dream. He said it could be their secret. He had the camera head looking out from the mansion and into the distance, like it was just about to go exploring the great unknown of the backwoods. Every time she'd look at it, it would be a cool reminder of all the cool things in the cosmos.

About half the students from Ricardo's dance class mingled in the backyard. Most crowded around him and Lucas, who sat on the few lawn chairs Cassia had found in the back garden shed. All the students had been invited to come over, but not everyone wanted to make the long drive.

Deputy Chester came as a fellow dance student, and not in uniform, instead wearing khakis and a blue button-down shirt. He happily talked to the redhead with curls Cassia had seen him dancing with in some of their classes. Cassia made a note to herself to learn the woman's name. There were too many students Cassia did not know yet, but she knew it was a good problem to have, especially with so many of them here, in her home.

Her home!

Cassia struggled to keep the silly smile off her face.

She did at least remember Mark's name, who this time sported a hand-knit sweater in a fancy pattern of black and brown. It was beginning to click with her that Mark had probably knitted them all himself.

Even Deputy Katelin Porter was there, grabbing the last of the pretzels out of the bowl on the large table they had set up out back. She stood next to Cassia and watched Jane play a strange game of fetch with Miss Mansfield. Miss Mansfield would bat a ball across the yard and Jane would run and fetch it. Cassia wasn't going to be the one to say anything about the game.

"I can't believe Jane thought all that bad stuff was going to happen if she told the truth," Katelin said. Katelin had vehemently admonished Cassia to call her Katelin when she was out of uniform, and not Deputy Porter. Today was an out of uniform day.

"Yeah. It was pretty brutal. Polina tried to grab the kid, but Jane ducked and ran. If Polina hadn't been wearing those stupid high heels, she might not have hit the railing and fallen from the building."

"Why did they think they could pin it on Ricardo?" Katelin

asked. She had worked with Deputy Waters for almost five years, but when he was taken out of the department, it was almost like an oath of silence had been taken. Cassia knew more about what happened than Katelin did.

"I guess he thought he could just show the one section of the video with Ricardo going into the back and Polina not coming out again. His plan was to destroy the rest of the tapes. Especially the one with Polina slipping and falling when the railing gave way. Thank goodness for great backup systems," Cassia said.

"I'm not so sure Waters would agree," Katelin said.

"Is this the girls' section? Can I join?" Genevieve said as she sidled up between the two of them. Despite the full spread of goodies on the table, Genevieve had her old favorite sandwich in hand. Pimento loaf. Cassia could smell the mustard and pimentos from a foot away.

"Yes, and yes," Cassia said.

"You need to go shopping," Genevieve said. "You're almost out of mustard."

"Doesn't that mean *you* need to take me shopping?" Cassia asked. Katelin watched, bemused.

"Sure. Whatever," Genevieve said around a mouthful of food. "Do you know what I found out?"

Katelin and Cassia shook their heads.

"That Ricardo is more of a softie than I ever suspected. He agreed to do all that movie stuff because Jane's mother had not done well with all his traveling for work, so he'd promised to do better with his next family."

"Even with an ex?" Cassia asked, incredulous.

Genevieve shrugged her shoulders. "Guilt can make you do terrible things, I guess. Plus, that Polina woman was a master at manipulation."

Cassia lifted her eyebrows and stared meaningfully at Genevieve.

"What?" Genevieve asked in mock innocence.

Cassia tilted her head. She wasn't giving in on this one.

"Oh, alright, alright. Point for you," Genevieve said, throwing up her hands in mock surrender before turning away. "You like my manipulations," she muttered as she walked away.

"What?" Cassia called loudly.

"Nothing," Genevieve yelled back over her shoulder.

Katelin smirked next to Cassia, not at all disturbed by their teasing. "I'll go make sure she doesn't get into too much trouble," Katelin said with a wink as she followed Genevieve to the refreshment table.

"Hello," Nate Perauski called from around the side of the mansion. He walked towards the group in the back while holding the hand of a tiny woman next to him. The woman would have been short in any circumstances, but next to his nearly seven foot height, it almost looked comical. Her smile was brilliant, perfectly fitting her elfin looks.

"Hi," Cassia called, going to meet them.

"Cassia, this is my wife, Madison," Nate said.

"Hi, Cassia," Madison said. She smiled at Cassia, her brilliant blue eyes charming Cassia from the start. With her trendy short pixie haircut, and stylish clothes, Cassia thought it was only a matter of seconds before Genevieve spotted her and came swooping in to make a new friend.

"Welcome!" Cassia said, thrilled that they made it to her party.

"Wouldn't miss it," Nate said. "You know how small town life goes."

A month ago, she would have thought that saying small town life was an insult, but now Cassia was starting to think it wasn't one after all.

She looked at all the new people in her yard and had a strange and fuzzy feeling she couldn't actually remember

SHAW COLLINS

before. It felt terrifyingly wonderful. Glowing, even, to have all these people here.

"Yes, I'm starting to figure that out," Cassia said, turning back to Nate. She waved them over to the refreshment table. "Oh, wait, before I forget," Cassia said, calling after Nate. "Are we still on for next Tuesday?"

Nate paused, then nodded, remembering. "Oh, yes. Your New York law firm call. I still don't know why you want me in on it."

"Because I trust you," Cassia said with a laugh. "I'm not so sure about them."

Nate nodded. "Maybe we'll have more records from the bank before then too."

That would be great. Cassia really wanted to get to the bottom of where her aunt's money had gone. Perhaps the New York people would know. In any case, she wasn't lying about trusting Nate. It would be good to have him helping her.

Then Sheriff Andrews walked into the party, wearing a tight pair of dockers and an even tighter polo. He looked both very good and very strange out of uniform. He glanced around awkwardly.

Cassia hadn't really expected him to show up, but a part of her was definitely pleased to see him, even if he only shared his smiles with Jane.

She went to go greet him.

210

ALSO BY SHAW COLLINS

CASSIA LEMON MYSTERIES

Cat on a Wire

Cat Dancer

Cat and Mouse

———

www.ShawCollins.com